THE ZONE

#1

HARD TARGET

Books by James Rouch

The Zone Series
#1:   Hard Target
#2:   Blind Fire
#3:   Hunter Killer
#4:   Sky Strike
#5:   Overkill
#6:   Plague Bomb
#7:   Killing Ground
#8:   Civilian Slaughter
#9:   Body Count
#10: Death March

World War II Collection
#1:   The War Machines
#2:   Tiger
#3:   Gateway to Hell

THE ZONE

#1

HARD TARGET

James Rouch

SPEAKING VOLUMES, LLC

NAPLES, FLORIDA

2012

THE ZONE

HARD TARGET # 1

ISBN 978-1-61232-903-1

International Press Services. Dateline 22nd July.
Timed 09.34 GMT. Transmission Clearance Number:
8442/220786.

For   All newsdesks.
Source   Official. Special release by Press Office—
*   Supreme   Headquarters,   Allied   Powers,*
*   Europe. 09.13 GMT. This dateline. Text*
*   confirmation.   SHAPE P.R. Office 09.21*
*   GMT.*

Suitable for immediate inclusion stop-press.

On the eve of the second anniversary of the outbreak of
World War III, Russian ground forces have for the
fourth time this year used fractional kT nuclear
weapons in an attempt to extend the central sector of
the War Zone, launching an armoured thrust towards
Frankfurt. First reports indicate six warheads em-
ployed; estimated individual kilotonnage between
point-one and point-three. NATO forces unable to use

nuclear demolition devices to contain attack, due to presence of refugee columns being used by the Communists as cover for their troop movements.

A counter strike by elements of the American 3rd Armoured Division and West German 5th Infantry Division has checked the Warsaw Pact advance at Aschaffenburg. Enemy losses are put at ninety-seven tanks, one hundred and twenty-two other armoured fighting vehicles, including a number of tracked missile systems. NATO casualties not yet confirmed but stated, unofficially, to be acceptable. Heavy fighting continues.

Fighting in the Northern Sector of the Zone remains at a low level for the second week. Intelligence reports suggest that the Warsaw Pact forces are still regrouping and re-equipping after the heavy losses they sustained when they failed to pinch out the British-held Hanover salient, in June.

For the first time since their mutinies on the opening day of the war, East German troops have been identified in the front line, near Wolfsberg in Austria. Their presence in that quiet area is taken as an indication that some elements of the GDR forces, after the purges, are now being rehabilitated.

Additions to Official approved list of reference sources for expansion or features.
THE WAR ZONE: A SCAR ACROSS EUROPE. Steiner and Blackburn. A good general background. With maps.
PAWNS OF POLITICS. Doder and Doder, N.Y. A

study of the refugee problem inside the Zone.

THE THORN THAT SLOWED THE BEAR. New English Library. A crystal-clear analysis of the cumulative consequences of the GDR revolt on the first day of the war. Presented in dramatised form. Compiled from official Intelligence reports, and the only coherent work on the subject.

THE U.S. WAR MACHINE
THE SOVIET WAR MACHINE
SOVIET AIR POWER.
Salamander. Lavishly illustrated guides to the principal combatants' armed forces. Cover strategy as well as hardware. Comprehensive fact files.

Chapter One

The Russian T84 tank was advancing through the last wisps of the yellow chemical fog at a cautious walking pace. Its broad tracks created hardly a ripple in the poisonous ochre puddles on the surface of the narrow road winding between the blighted fields. In turn the long snout of its cannon, and the twin rocket launchers mounted above it, covered a wide arc of ground to either side of its route, as the low dome-shaped turret constantly swivelled back and forth.

Corporal Howard wiped a smear of mud from the field-radar's display screen and called a reading. "Range is two-thousand now, Sarge. He's hardly moving, still holding the same course. When are we going to clobber him?"

At the far end of the short turf-roofed trench, one of the three men crouched around an improvised card table sat back and took a long hard look at his hand. It was the best Sergeant Hyde had been dealt all morning. His eyes, looking out of a caricature of a face that the plastic surgeons had given up on long ago, flickered once to signal his annoyance at the interruption. None of the other fire-welded components of his features were capable of registering as much. He kept his voice casual, so as not to give anything away to the other players.

"We'll give them a bit longer. Give me a shout when it's down to twelve hundred, or if they change course or speed. Your bid, Libby."

Unlike the section's senior NCO, Private Libby had welcomed the interruption, hoping it would terminate the game early. He hated playing poker with Hyde. It wasn't the man's ghastly appearance, he'd grown used to that: what he disliked so intensely was the unnatural advantage the sergeant enjoyed in having that expressionless mask.

"One hundred marks." It was reckless, too much when he only held a pair of kings, but sod it, he'd love to out-bluff the bloody monster just this once.

The third player, Private Collins, kept his eyes glued to his cards without really seeing them. All he wanted to do was avoid looking at Hyde. He'd grabbed at the chance when the sergeant had invited him to sit in, it being virtually the first time anyone had spoken to him in the three days since he'd joined the unit, except to shout an order. And now he fumbled with his cards, forgetting the little he knew of the game as he fought to conceal his revulsion at Hyde's appearance.

More than the light needed to conduct their game was let in by the crude roof of their shelter. Collins jumped at the sound of an explosion some distance away.

"Sit still." Libby immediately regretted the sharp note of irritation in his voice, as Hyde upped the betting again.

Howard brushed a worm from the top of the set. "Just a stray shell, or some poor bugger stepping on a mine. Nothing for you to worry about. You'll get used to it." He glanced at the chemical-level indicator fixed to the wall of the trench. The band of changing colour had edged a fraction further along the strip of sensitized paper. "Pity it isn't all high-explosive. I'm fed up with this stinking chemical shit Ivan keeps chucking about."

Now the fuzzy red dot working its way down from the top of the green-tinted screen was beginning to pulsate, and pale symbols flashed along the bottom of the grid-marked display. The corporal pursed his lips, turned two of the set's three dials and with practiced ease made quick sense of the numbers that came up.

"The Ruskies in that tin can out there are using detectors."

"What sort?" Hyde didn't bother to look up.

"Electro-magnetic."

Hyde grunted, and continued to scrutinise his cards.

Collins, on his first active patrol, found it impossible to affect the same casual air as the others. There was none of the tension or drama he'd expected. Nor the state of alertness that his instructors had demanded of him in every exercise during his basic training, and on the demolition course he'd subsequently attended. All that was totally lacking in these combat veterans.

There was another explosion, much closer than the last. The corporal swore, thumped the side of the radar set and swore again.

"Trigger-happy shits. They've clobbered the bloody dish. We're blind."

11

Hyde fanned out his hand to reveal a full house of jacks and queens, pocketed the modest pile of coins and notes and went over to join Howard. "Your gadget might be, but I'm not. Move over, I'll take the bugger on visual."

He knelt on the compacted soil at the bottom of the excavation and pressed his face against the rubber surround of their periscope sight. Friction peeled a flake of purple scar tissue from his brow. He gradually adjusted the magnification until the stencilled red stars on the tank's turret stood out clearly, as did the slapped-on illegible slogans on its skirts of side armour. He lined up the cross hairs of the sight on the front of the tank at the base of its turret.

"Right, I've got him. Transfer control."

Howard unlooped an extension cable from the back of the radar set and plugged its loose end into the small black box attached to the side of the periscope. A pea-bulb flashed green to signal a good connection and the state of the batteries.

"It's all yours, Sarge."

"Let's cook some Commies, then." Hyde's left thumb strayed to the end of the periscope handle and flipped open a hinged yellow cap to reveal a red button set in the shallow recess beneath it. The thumb hovered for a moment, then crushed down.

At the fringe of a copse of defoliated oaks, a hundred yards to the right of the trench, there was a brief stab of flame as a sharp-nosed broad finned rocket jumped from the ground. A moment later, a longer flame spurted from the rear of the anti-tank missile as it accelerated towards its target.

Five seconds into its flight and three-quarters of its

journey completed, the missile veered suddenly to the left, lurched back almost on to course, then turned again more sharply and tumbled out of the air. A plume of soil and smoke marked its point of impact.

"The sods are jamming us. Give me an old-fashioned wire-guided system any day." Hyde jabbed his finger at the corporal. "You're the wizard with these bloody gadgets. We've got one round left, rig it so those fuckers can't knock it down."

While Howard broke a seal to open a small inspection panel on the side of the black box, the sergeant kept tracking the Soviet vehicle.

Already made cautious by the radar location dish they had detected and destroyed, and now alarmed by the abortive attack, the crew of the T84 played safe, and rather than use the tank's exceptional high speed to escape, drove it into cover. Amid a cloud of grey exhaust from its V12 diesel, it backed through the remains of a hedge and took up a position among the gaunt soot-stained walls of what had once been a half-timbered barn. Twice in swift succession, white fire tipped the snout of its cannon and balls of flame roared through the naked oaks, starting blazes among the heaped brown leaves and peeling trunks.

"That should do it." Howard moved out of Hyde's way. "It'll take faster reflexes and better electronic countermeasures than that Commie crew has got, to stop the next one."

"I hope you're right." Libby was putting away the cards, making ready for a hurried departure. "I'd hate to get smeared all over the Hanover salient just because you got a couple of wires crossed."

"It'll work." Howard's tone suggested that he

13

resented the implied slur.

"Give it a rest, you two." Hyde pulled his face away from the viewfinder. The edge of the rubber had left an indentation in the spongy tissue of his multiple grafts, a bizarre pattern that circled his eyes. "Save your bickering for later." He took up position again.

This time a missile jumped and fled from a patch of sickly yellow bracken, and for the first two and a half seconds of its flight executed the same pre-programmed gentle evasive manoeuvres as its unsuccessful predecessor. Then it soared almost vertically into the low cloud and disappeared.

From bitter painful experience Hyde knew the panic the Russian tank men would be feeling at that moment, as the rocket's violent change of course jerked it off the screen of their hostile-fire locator an instant before they could take effective measures against it. Even, if they kept their heads there was nothing they could do now, it was even too late to bale out.

Ignoring every distraction, the sergeant kept the crossed black filaments of the periscope sight locked firmly on to the small portion of dusty armour that was all he could see of the T84, tucked away among the distant piles of rubble.

At a height of four hundred feet above the tank, the missile's own seeker system detected the vehicle's metal mass and engine noise. It was already diving to rejoin the line-of-sight flight path dictated by the command unit in the trench, and only had to fractionally steepen the angle of its five-hundred-mile-an-hour descent to deliver its lethal cargo to the vulnerably thin armour of the T84's engine deck.

Nine pounds of shaped explosive charge, generating

a colossal temperature, blasted the engine from its mounts and punched through an internal bulkhead to project a stream of vaporised steel into the crew compartment, setting off every round of ammunition in the automatic loader simultaneously.

Seconds after the muted echo of the explosion, the men in the trench felt the faint, short-lived tremor of the shock wave.

"Well, don't bloody hang about, then. We're out of missiles and those buggers might have squawked for help before we took them apart."

It didn't need Hyde's urging to speed up the rate at which the equipment was being made into compact loads for carrying. Collins would have helped, but every time he thought of a job he could do it was already being done, and usually faster and better than he could have managed. He could only watch in amazement as the sergeant wrenched the periscope from the trench wall, stamped it into scrap and then pulled earth down to bury it completely.

Libby saw the expression of incredulous disbelief on Collins' face, and winked at him. "It's on limited issue for evaluation, field modifications aren't allowed. We take it back with the seals broken . . ." He made a cutting motion with his finger across his throat. "Better to mark it down as lost in action."

As Hyde reached up to remove a section of the turf roof, a grotesque figure plunged through, bringing it all down. The unexpected arrival tore off his respirator so that it hung down by one strap across the front of his anti-contamination suit, and jabbed the long slim barrel of a sniper's rifle into Hyde's stomach. The powerful weapon looked top-heavy with its mass of complicated sighting aids. As the sergeant swept the rifle aside the intruder glowered at him, his face colouring with the intensity of emotion that he had difficulty finding words to express.

"You rotten bugger. You fucking ugly bastard. You've done it again, you scar-faced lump of shit."

Libby tugged at the rifleman's arm. "Take it easy, Clarence."

The sniper wrenched himself free. He didn't bring the Enfield up again, but his blazing eyes stayed locked on Hyde. "You knew I was bloody out there and what did you do, you blew those cruddy Reds to atoms. How can I get a crack at them if they don't bale out of those tin cans? What am I supposed to do, take pot shots at the pieces flying through the air?"

There was no outward reaction from the sergeant. Collins watched, waiting for the answering blast and string of charges. None came.

Hyde shrugged. "You can always stay and wait for the next one if you want. Suit yourself." With that, he climbed out and began to walk away.

Clarence went bright red. He whirled round, aiming at Hyde's back. His finger tightened on the trigger and, as it did, he jerked the barrel upwards and pumped five fast shots into the sky over the sergeant's head. Hyde never flinched, simply kept on walking. The action appeared to dissipate the sniper's rage, and after a moment he reluctantly tagged along at the back of the file as the others left the trench and followed their sergeant.

By putting on a spurt Collins caught up with Libby.

"How come the sarge lets him get away with that?" He kept his voice low. "I'd have gone inside for the rest of me natural for one tenth of that back at basic training camp."

"Takes a lot to get the sarge going, in fact I've never seen him lose his rag yet. He don't frighten easy either, he hasn't got a nerve in his body." Libby didn't bother to copy the precaution of whispering. "As for Clarence, I reckon he's off his head, a bit at least. Has been ever since a flak-damaged Tupolev came down on his wife and kids in married quarters in Cologne. He was on his way there on a forty-eight hour when it happened, arrived home just in time to pull out what was left of them. He doesn't talk about it, must have been messy. Anyway, now all he lives for is killing Ivans. He's good at it." He called back to the sniper. "How many is it now, Clarence?"

"One hundred and ninety-two." There was no hint of pride or boasting in the matter-of-fact announcement. The sniper went on slotting fresh cartridges into a magazine.

"See what I mean? He's good."

Back in the trench it had come as a shock to Collins to hear the torrent of obscenity from the usually quiet and reserved man, but this . . . Of course he knew his speciality, but he'd never realised . . . nearly two hundred . . . it was incredible. Clarence, with his neat and fussy ways and his quiet distaste for the crudities of army life . . . nearly two hundred!

". . . was due to go on an officer-training course, but he had a breakdown and was lucky to stay in at all."

Collins realised with a start that Libby was still talking. He made non-committal noises to give the

17

impression he'd heard every word.

". . . Now when he gets leave, he goes back there and sits all the time in the garden of remembrance where their ashes are scattered. One week of grief keeps him killing for six months."

Their skin was prickling, and their eyes watered and smarted with the concentration of chemicals in the air. Even up-wind of the saturated area, and despite the prophylactics they had taken, the noxious substances still affected their respiration and made breathing both difficult and painful. It was a temptation to run, to get to the sanctuary of their air-conditioned transport as quickly as possible, but that would have been fatal with the high level of toxic material in the atmosphere.

Whole chunks of the landscape through which they trudged looked as if they had been bleached. What little greenery there still was had a blotched and leprous look. The sky, filled with the dust and smoke of two years' bitter conflict, was a uniform dull red that betrayed no hint of the sun's position, but trapped its light and spread a meagre portion of it across the alien landscape.

The angular turret-topped hull of the skimmer was a welcome sight when they reached the gorse-shrouded gully. Burke, their combat driver, was waiting.

"Burke by name, and burk by bloody nature." Hyde dropped his pack heavily on to the older man's feet. "You might have turned it round ready for a quick getaway if it were needed. Or doesn't your weary old brain stretch to such mind-boggling initiative?"

Burke scowled, and heaved the kit through the open door set in the hovercraft's front, beside the driver's position. "I might have done, but an Ivan sky-spy was

18

pissing about overhead earlier, so I thought I'd better keep the Iron Cow as cool as possible, in case it was doing an infra-red survey." He patted the faded name painted on the starboard hull front.

"You've always got a ruddy answer, haven't you?"

The sergeant's sarcasm made no impression on Burke. He clambered aboard to take his seat.

Last to board was Corporal Howard. He carefully stowed the field-radar set, before threading his way down the narrow single compartment of the craft's interior to the built-in radar console at the rear. The instant he activated the complex electronic systems and put on his headset, the front ramp lifted drawbridge-like to seal the doorway and the twin Allison turbofan engines on either side of the crew compartment whined into life.

Burke tapped a proportion of their combined two-and-a-half-thousand horsepower for the lift ducts, and the concertinaed skirts about the hull's lower edge straightened, bulged and rose from the ground as they lifted the fifteen-ton machine.

As the skimmer whirled round almost in its own length, Libby hauled himself into the cramped cannon-armed turret set in the centre of the roof. Hyde sat immediately behind their driver in the command seat, while Clarence leant back on a bench and began to clean his rifle. Only Collins sat bolt upright in the approved and official manner, feet firmly on the floor, heels against the locker under his seat, rump pressed back hard into the angle made by the metal wall of the compartment and the thinly padded bench top. The general purpose machine gun he'd been given the dubious honour of carrying and caring for was between

19

his knees, butt on floor, barrel tip beneath his nose. His satchel of demolition charges, still intact, rested on the seat beside him.

Unlike Clarence, Collins had not been unhappy to see the Russian tank so comprehensively destroyed. He wanted more time to get used to being in action before he took on the task for which he'd trained, finishing off disabled enemy tanks capable of being salvaged and sent back into battle.

After a casual glance at an external contamination monitor, Clarence turned up the air-conditioning to one and a half pounds of positive pressure. "The wind must have shifted. It's as thick as porridge out there."

Collins managed to eliminate most of the discomfort by swallowing hard several times, but his ears continued to "pop" at irregular intervals. Looking forward, he could see the tattered remains of the wiper blades scraping clear arcing tracks across the thick front-vision block.

"There's a beam on us." Howard's shout echoed through the alloy cocoon, adding fresh discomfort to their ears.

"Identify." Hyde's response was as punishing.

"Acoustic."

Several actions in the cramped compartment blended into a single confused tangle of movement. Clarence grabbed a pair of garishly painted grenades from a rack and fired them in rapid sequence from a short barrelled discharger set in the roof behind the turret: Hyde hurled himself towards Collins, shoved him aside and smashed his fist down hard on a large orange stud, one of a colour-coded row.

Simultaneously, the nose of the craft dipped as

Burke lifted the forward edge of the skirt to gain every ounce of speed. The skimmer surged ahead in response as the engines screamed up to full emergency power.

The feeling of tightness in the muscles of his face, the sudden dryness in his mouth, had nothing to do with Collins' fear of the consequences of Burke's manic evasive driving. He knew, as did the others, that somewhere out there a Russian infiltrator had spotted them and was, at that very moment guiding down on their heads an anti-tank missile or shell. There were only seconds . . .

Hyde's urgent action had released a knobbly fibre-glass box from the outside of the hull. It tumbled down the camouflage-painted metal, bounced from the engine pod to the puffed-out wall of the ride-skirt and landed on a tangled mat of rotting vegetation. An instant later it came to rest. Telescopic aerials lanced from it and began to broadcast a blast of white noise that would continue until its powerpack was rapidly exhausted, or until it successfully decoyed an enemy warhead riding down the beam focused on the Iron Cow.

In the air above it, the two grenades Clarence had launched rocketed back and forth, giving off dense clouds of exhaust-simulating smoke. Both produced a whining scream that mimicked the full-thrust engine noise of the fast disappearing hovercraft. From the tails of both spewed a series of flares and incendiary pellets, whose combustion temperature dwarfed the shielded infra-red signature of the twin Allison turbofans.

They weren't needed. Just twelve seconds into its

21

short life the squawk-box was almost reduced to its component molecules by a Soviet AT-12 anti-tank missile.

Deafened by the howl of their straining power units, Hyde had no way of knowing if their ruse had worked until Burke leapt the speeding skimmer over a shallow ridge, and into the safety of low ground surrounded by rolling hills.

The vehicle's speed fell to a saner pace and they began to drive between serried rows of weed-infested rubble. The battered hulks of rusting cars and trucks and a few drunkenly leaning telegraph poles were the only recognisable features of what had once been a prosperous outer suburb of Hanover.

Burke dropped the speed still further, to cut down the dust raised by their progress and give the perimeter sensors of their battalion's intruder alarm system time to identify them.

Ahead of them loomed the outline of a gutted local shopping centre. Its precast concrete fabric, though blackened and warped by the fires that had raged through it, had survived largely intact. Only a handful of the less robust surrounding buildings had stood up to the repeated bombing and shelling of the area. Most had been levelled by blast and fire, or been reduced to ragged roofless shells.

Moving at a crawl, the Iron Cow nosed into one of the shop fronts, the dangling remnants of neon signs brushing and grating on its roof as it did. The engines were cut and it drifted into the heart of the building, settling to rest inside an enclosure formed of suspended plastic sheeting.

Slow-moving figures shuffled forward, their outlines

made indistinct in the gloom by the cumbersome heavy-duty anti-contamination suits and respirators they wore. Each of the apparitions waved the spray-emitting nozzle of a hose in front of him.

Activated bleach slurry ran from the hull, flushing from every crevice the last of any persistent chemicals adhering to it. That done, the skimmer was scalded clean with high pressure steam jets. A member of the decontamination crew tapped on the driver's vision block and gave a slow motion thumbs-up to the men inside.

There was no rush to leave the cramped quarters. Hyde and his men just sat there, letting the tension drain from them.

Collins declined the tobacco pouch and paper that Burke offered him. "No, thanks, I don't. Are all the patrols like that?"

It was Corporal Howard who took it on himself to answer, when no one else did. "They're all different, but that was an easy one, if that's what you mean."

"Think we'll be getting a spot of leave, Sarge?" Burke made a critical examination of the butt he held, then puffed vigorously to keep the last shreds of tobacco alight.

"What's the matter?" Libby came down from the turret seat. "Don't you like your work?"

"Fuck the work," Burke growled. "I'm just saying it'd be nice to have something to look forward to when we got back."

The slit in the face of Sergeant Hyde that lips would have marked as a mouth barely opened as he spoke. "I've got a feeling the CO will have something waiting for us, but it won't be a seventy-two-hour pass."

23

Chapter Two

"I don't give a fuck what you think of the plan, just make the shitty thing work." Colonel Lee Lippincott took the well-chewed pencil stub from between his perfectly capped teeth and spat out shreds of wood. "The orders say this is a joint operation with the British, and as I'll be the bastard catching shit from the Liaison Staff if you screw up, then believe me you'd better not screw up. If you do, and make it back, then you'll be fucking lucky to end up as a private third class, testing piss as a beer substitute."

Major Revell waited until Ol' Foul Mouth had finished flecking the floor to the right of his chair with another spattering of spittle and splinters. No effort he could have made would have kept the edge out of his voice, so he didn't try. "OK, so this British tank-hunter squad know the ground, and the whole crazy idea comes from a smart-arse Staff Officer in Brussels, who wants an example of successful cooperation between us and them to counter stories of friction in the press back home. But why, just tell me why, a Commie tank repair

25

shop is so damned important all of a sudden."

"Shit, we've been in the salient for two weeks now, helping bolster the British defences, you know the picture." Lippincott picked flakes of blue paint from his fleshy lips and examined them on the ends of his fingers. "After the balls-up they made of trying to clear this pocket in June, Soviet 2nd Guards ain't exactly the Russian High Command's favourite outfit. Rumour has it they came close to losing their fancy title. They're going to have to try again, but they ain't getting much in the way of new equipment. As things stand we about match them in armour, but somehow they've got their cruddy hands on this crack workshop unit. If their tanks are in prime condition when the show starts again, fitted with the latest mods, it could make all the difference."

"If we know where it is then drop a cruise on it; why send a platoon of my men on a suicide mission?"

A parody of a benevolent grin creased the colonel's rubbery features. "Suicide is when you die by choice, Major; you ain't got none." He read the expression on the young officer's deeply sunburnt face, and the grin faded. Hell, Revell gave him the creeps; couldn't take a joke, never laughed, lived like a damned monk: Jesus, he wasn't normal. "We don't have the exact location, it's just somewhere around Gifhorn. That's a no-go area, stiff with stinking refugees. If we kill so much as a scabby kraut goat I get stick from above, so area weapons are out, saturation, conventional or nuclear."

"When the hell are we going to stop fighting this war with our damned hands tied behind our backs?" Revell crashed his palms down on the desk top between them.

26

"Why is it always us who have to be the nice guys? It's time to hit the Reds hard with everything we've got."

"Don't fucking shout at me, Major." Revell's outburst had made Ol' Foul Mouth jump and now he shouted back. "You think I don't know how we're hamstrung. I'm up to my fucking arse in directives that originate from shitty do-gooding pressure groups in Germany and England and back in the States. I'd like nothing better than to put aside for each of them a share of the barrel of super-napalm I fancy pouring over the head of every last torturing Commie."

Lippincott rose half out of his seat, hammering his desk with his fist at every word. "In the Balkans we were fighting Slavs, Bulgarians, even bloody Cubans, tough cruds, dirty even; but compared with 2nd Guards, they're bloody choirboys. 2nd Guards are animals, the lowest; you lift up pigshit and that's where you'll find them. They tore up the rules two years ago, but our politicians haven't heard that yet, so while the Reds do what they like we have to look twice before we so much as chuck a grenade. But at least you get to smash them sometimes—I fucking don't."

Revell saw the pinned-up sleeve over the stump of the colonel's left arm and read the bitterness and frustration in his voice. He lowered his own when he spoke again, but every word was punched out sharp and clear.

"Smash them? All we're ever allowed to do is carry out a few raids, maybe lay an ambush or two. The rest of the time we sit in holes in the ground waiting for the next mass Commie attack. We should be taking the war to them in a big way, tearing their eyes out, not

27

pecking at them."

"Not a fucking chance." With a neatly manicured nail Lippincott prised a sliver of soggy wood from between his top teeth and flicked it to a far corner of the office. "You don't think our cruddy political bosses want us to start winning, do you? Shit, no. Of course they'll dole out just enough hardware to let us hold the Reds, and on occasion enough to enable us to mount division strength attacks, with limited objectives of course, to keep up morale and give the newsboys some fresh footage—but they sure as hell don't want us to start pushing the Commies right back. If that happened, the Reds might be tempted to break that cosy little hot-line agreement and take the war outside the Zone. None of those skunk-faced rats in Westminster or on Capitol Hill want any nukes falling in their back garden."

"You want me to tell my men that? You want me to tell them we've a job to do, bu we mustn't do it too well?"

"Don't get smart, Major. This mission *is* important. The Hanover salient is our last chance to deny the Reds a straight run to Essen and the Ruhr and the Channel. You knock out that workshop, screw up 2nd Guards Army, and you'll buy us more time to consolidate."

From the top of a stack of papers in his in-tray the colonel took a type-written sheet and waved it in front of Revell. "No, it ain't a new brand of arse wiper, it's a note from a two-star general. He says the press will be getting this story. They'll be encouraged to make a big splash about British-American cooperation if the mission goes well. Now I ain't about to disappoint a two-star general, so don't balls it up. No friction, understand? I want everything to go as smoothly as a well-oiled cock up a nice slack fanny, or else . . ."

Libby's fist hit PFC Dooley a solid blow in the gut. As he fell to his knees the big American lunged forward and, catching his opponent by surprise, brought him down too. Before Libby could regain his feet Dooley was on him and the breath whistled from them as they pounded each other.

"What the bloody hell is going on here? Break it up." Corporal Howard pushed through the tight circle of men that had formed around the combatants and was then in turn pushed aside by his sergeant.

At that moment the more powerfully built American was on top, hands locked about Libby's throat. Hyde hesitated a fraction of a second, undecided which was the best way to end the fight without giving grounds for further aggravation between the Americans and his men. But even as he stepped forward to pull them apart himself, Major Revell came through the crowd on the far side and instantly delivered a savagely powerful chop to the back of Dooley's neck.

Eyes bulging, tongue protruding between teeth half-hidden by foam, he began to topple to the floor. His fall was arrested by the officer, who grabbed his ears and hauled him to his feet.

Revell spoke quietly, never taking his intense pale blue eyes from the semi-conscious man's face. In the general silence the words carried to everyone there.

"Listen to me, Dooley. The colonel said 'no friction', you understand?"

The soldier went cross-eyed, attempted to shake his

head, winced and nodded.

"One warning only on this one. I know you, Dooley. It happens again and you'll be doing mine clearance with a jack-hammer, OK?"

Dooley's knees had gone rubbery and only the officer's tight grip kept him upright. He nodded, again with the same painful result.

Letting go his hold, Revell turned to Hyde. "Any idea what all this was about?"

"No, Major." Hyde shook his head. "No idea at all, but it won't happen again." By Christ it wouldn't, he wasn't going to be shown up in front of an officer from another unit, American, British or whatever. But especially not in front of this one. Although he'd so far had little contact with the American forces that made up half the NATO troops fighting in Europe, he had in his mind's eye a composite image of a typical Yank officer. Revell didn't fit it at all.

The three hovercraft personnel carriers that would carry them on their mission were almost ready. Sergeant Hyde suspected that the flare-up had occurred as a result of Dooley's constant attempts to pilfer pieces of equipment from the Iron Cow. Libby and Burke had spent weeks gathering together a complete set of accessories for their transport, from wrecks and other unofficial sources and Libby in particular had been steadily growing more irritated with the big American's jackdaw tendencies.

Revell sat on a packing case, occasionlly glancing at the map board resting in his lap, but most of the time watching the final preparations going on about the skimmers. Working conditions inside the ruined block of shops that served as a camouflaged company HQ and vehicle repair shed were appalling. The air was permeated with the stench of bleach that failed to lay the taint of cordite from the frequent conventional long-range bombardment missiles with which the Russians pounded the salient. There was only such natural light as filtered in to work by—the generator had been.yet another casualty of the current spares shortage—and the floor was littered with debris, grease and broken glass.

Casually, on the transparent cover of the map of northern Germany, the major drew a broad arrow with his blue marker pen, from their present position five miles east of the centre of Hanover, to a point about thirty miles closer to the old East German border, near Gifhorn. He looked at the line, so easy to draw, taking only a second to do. How long would the real journey take, racing from one piece of safe ground to another, constantly probing for holes in the Russians' network of ground surveillance radars? It would take all of the remaining few hours of darkness to reach the target area. Most of the way they would be traveling through territory controlled by the Russians. There were gaps in the defences, but the deeper they went the harder the gaps would be to find, and with radio silence ordered they could expect no help if they ran into trouble, and the chances were that they would.

There would have to be ten minutes set aside for a final briefing, it certainly wouldn't take longer than that. They had their weapons, a mission and a circle on a map. And that was it.

For two weeks his men had been holding defensive positions, with nothing to do but grow bored and become irritable. And now suddenly it was all rush

31

again. All the preparations for a mission that called for meticulous planning were having to be completed in eight hours.

"We've finished loading now, sir."

Revell looked up. Master Sergeant Windle was standing casually in front of him. Good dependable old Windle, with the emphasis on old. He should have been rotated back to the States a year ago, but he'd played on the shortage of experienced sergeants, and wangled one extension after another. Still, while Windle was around, all was well. He'd come through so many actions without a scratch that the men had begun to believe he was immortal and regarded him as the embodiment of their luck. It was a theory that the next thirty-six hours would put severely to the test.

"OK, have everyone muster by Hyde's skimmer. Was there something else?" From Windle's perceptible hesitation before turning away he knew there was.

"This British bunch, Major." Windle needed no second opening. "Their sergeant's got a face like the phantom of the opera; their driver is the laziest creep I ever set eyes on, and the one who goes round with a sniper rifle substituting for a security blanket, well he's off his head."

"Are you saying we . . . *you* can't work with them?"

"No, sir, that's not what I'm saying, it's just that . . ."

"Listen, maybe we've been too insular, too self-contained for too long. Take a real look at our men; Dooley and that mercurial temperament of his, and Nelson with that doll . . ."

"His mascot, sir."

". . . and Cohen, he believes in Martians."

"He says that's because he's given up believing in the

human race, sir."

"You get my point though. The main thing is these British are good, damned good or they wouldn't be coming with us. Now let's get this briefing over with." Revell eased his aching backside off the rough wood of the crate and followed the sergeant. Well, this would be the last of the preliminaries. In twenty minutes they would pull out, to have the benefit of last light when they passed through their own lines and then he would be doing what he did best, fighting.

Dooley was forced to admit, at least to himself, that the driver of the Iron Cow was good, damned good. Private Burke might be an all-time record gold-bricker, but Jesus, could he throw that thing around. For the first time since the major had told him he'd be travelling with him and Cohen in Hyde's skimmer he began to feel less unhappy. If he had to be going into battle again, and with the major they always seemed to be, then he might as well go in with a combat driver good enough to get them back out again.

The interior of the vehicle was lit by a dull red glow from a single bulb over Howard's radar console, and more faintly at the front end of the compartment by the pale green glow given off by the screen of the driver's image intensifier.

With most of the mission's stores on board, stacked in the narrow centre aisle, there was little room for the passenger's legs. Libby and Cohen had their feet up on cases of incendiary grenades.

There was little talking among the men sitting cramped together on the benches. The salient was behind them now. Ahead lay thirty miles of what was a free-fire zone after dark. Surveillance radars, intruder alarms and sophisticated night sights having made fighting after sunset a practical reality, had also just about brought it to an end.

At night the battlefield belonged to the technicians. One man at a console could do the job of fifty sentries, and could call down in seconds a weight of fire sufficient to halt and smash a regiment of tanks.

So Howard sat at his board, watching for active radars focused on them, ready to jam any he found, and monitoring the compact but powerful electronic devices the Iron Cow carried to blanket her own emissions and avoid their detection by enemy passive detectors. Most of the tasks were handled by the on-board computer, but the equipment could fail and then his speed of action would be their only protection.

Science had given Burke the means by which to drive at approaching the vehicle's top speed at night, but it could do nothing to smooth the route they were forced to take if they were to avoid the Russians' most likely points of concentration. War in the Zone was a giant game of hide-and-seek with a deadly booby prize for the losers. And so the three carriers wove a complex snaking course through the fields and woods, some-times taking to the beds of streams for a distance, mud and water splashing up their hulls and turning to puffs of steam in the exhaust from their turbines. At other times they would use a stretch of road or lane, and the hurtling trio would skim through an abandoned village or past a huddle of refugee shelters and slew back on to the fields beyond.

And that was the final horrific ingredient of the

Zone. Few of the civilians whose homes lay within it had moved out. Areas existed where rural life went on much as before, but they were shrinking green oases in a dying landscape. Many would willingly have gone, a lot had tried, but the population beyond the Zone's boundaries feared contamination; from the chemicals they knew were being used, from radiation brought about by the many small-yield tactical nuclear weapons that had been used, and most of all from the mythical bacterial weapons that featured so strongly in each new rumour: and so the civilians caught in the Zone were literally forced to stay.

It was the worst in the big camps in the north of the Zone. There civilisation had collapsed and even the armies avoided them, save as now when the Russians were using a settlement as cover for activities they didn't want disturbed.

Revell had been watching Clarence take the cartridges from a spare Enfield magazine and clean them one at a time, before inspecting and replacing them. He reached across and took one of the long slim bullets from the cloth in which they nestled, and held it up against the light. Two small nicks were visible, just below its pointed tip. "How long have you been using dum-dums?"

Clarence went on with his work, not bothering to look up. "Since I found out the Russians were using them, about three months. You don't approve?"

"My men have known a bit longer." Revell handed the round back. "We've been using them nearer six."

Tucked up in a corner, his slight frame wrapped in cumbersome body armour, Abe Cohen closed his eyes and tried to sleep. It wouldn't come. Hell, he felt awful, like his stomach was about to climb his throat and hurl itself out of his mouth complete, in one great heave. It was worse than being seasick. At least at sea there was some sort of regular motion; it was still horrible but at least you knew what was coming. These skimmers were something else. He hugged his arms across his stomach, not that he could feel the contact through an inch of laminated fibre-glass and metal mesh, and tried again. He didn't care how tough the job they were going to do was, he'd happily have taken on the whole of 2nd Guards Army if only it meant getting out of this bucking bucket.

"There was a beam on us then," Howard called out.

"Take what evasive action you have to, but stay on this general heading." Hyde had given their driver the order before he remembered the major. He looked to see the officer's reaction.

Revell understood, and nodded. "Don't forget we've got a brood bringing up the rear."

"Another one. The Ruskies are looking for us now." A tight skidding turn almost threw Howard from his seat.

If Burke was making life uncomfortable for Cohen, he was also making it very difficult for the distant Russian radar operators who were trying to pick them up and plot their course.

Hedges and fences collapsed before the skimmers' onslaught. A small group of houses that couldn't even be glorified by the name of village were grazed and shaken as the racing hovercrafts scraped by, using their outline as cover and to confuse the enemy radar.

It worked, but the gap had widened between the Iron Cow and the following vehicles. They chased after the

36

British craft, almost nose to tail, as their drivers pushed themselves to the limit to keep up with Burke's fast progress between the houses.

Seven hundred yards from the hamlet, from a spot not quite within the fringes of a plantation of pines, there was a rapid succession of stabs of light as a multi-barrelled Russian ZSU-23 anti-aircraft tank opened up with all four of its 23mm cannon. Tracer arced through the night towards the ill-spaced file of NATO machines.

Chapter Three

A fifty-round burst of mixed explosive and armour-piercing shells struck the side of a brick-built tractor shed in front of the leading American skimmer. Part of the structure's corrugated iron roof was blasted off, and the second vehicle of the racing pair had to plough through an avalanche of falling bricks and beams as the decayed fabric of the building collapsed into its path.

The enemy gun-layer made a fractional adjustment to his aim, and his second burst caught the tail-end vehicle of the file as it turned into a narrow alleyway between a row of houses and a church.

Six of the high velocity shells smashed into its port engine, two more gouged their way across the skimmer's roof behind the turret. An explosive round self-destructed amid a tangle of externally stowed equipment, sending saws and hawsers and shovel handles spinning away into the night. The last three armour-piercing shells plunged in through the vehicle's rear plate, between the engine exhausts, their impacts marked by showers of white sparks.

39

Its remaining engine screaming at full power the hovercraft, towing thick white smoke, careened through a wild tight turn and thundered into the front of a boarded-up store. Its speed took it right inside and clouds of dust hid where it came to rest. A massive explosion lifted the building and bright flame bubbled from every window. The roof sagged, and then the whole property crashed down to bury the wreck.

"You'll have to pull forward. I can't see the bugger."

Burke made no move to do as their turret gunner urged, and drive the Iron Cow from the cover of the derelict cottage so that Libby could retaliate with their cannon armament.

Revell was standing looking out of the command cupola, just forward of the main turret. He watched as the other remaining skimmer took up a position across the street, nestling against a row of deserted houses. "We're not going anywhere while he's out there."

Hyde had been watching the scanner console over Howard's shoulder. "Might be an idea to try though, Major. That flak tank is calling for help."

Revell surveyed the country ahead. It was half a mile to the next substantial cover, a belt of woodland flanking the road.

"Aw, Major," Dooley had been listening, "we ain't gonna get in a fire fight with a flak wagon, are we? Jesus, that thing fires four thousand rounds a minute. All we've got is one barrel against their four, and three-round clips against their belt feed."

Now that he had at last realised that they had stopped moving, Cohen began to take an interest in what was going on. "Yeah, and they've got micro-wave radar. So it's not too hot in the ground mode, but we ain't got any."

The mound of blazing rubble that marked where the last skimmer had come to rest illuminated a considerable and expanding area in the centre of the settlement. Buildings adjoining it were already steaming and were liable to add their fuel to the conflagration at any moment.

"I don't think we have any choice." Even as Revell made up his mind, there was a massive detonation and the cottage alongside dissolved inside a roaring ball of fire. Bricks and slates crashed on to their hull and turret and rained down in the road.

Two more similarly massive concussions cratered the road behind them and blasted out the end wall of the church.

There was just time to grab a handhold before, on the major's command, Burke sent the machine surging forward. Like the others, they knew that those first gigantic blasts were just the ranging shots, the precursors of a much larger salvo of 240mm rockets to come.

Through a rear-facing periscope Revell saw that Windle's skimmer, though slower off the mark, was following.

More of the huge fin-stabilised rockets began to fall as they cleared the last of the straggling buildings. The houses were torn apart, their roofs lifted off and their contents scattered across the streets and gardens. Trees and telegraph poles caught by the blast were scorched, shredded and toppled to the ground. The air was filled with flying leaves and whipping lengths of wire.

Libby opened up with the cannon an instant after the last obstructing corner of a house was cleared, so fast it seemed he could hardly have had time to sight his target, let alone take aim.

Slower by a couple of seconds, the flak tank replied to the three armour-piercing incendiary rounds sent against it with a ripple of twenty of its own.

The skimmer's wild gyrations, as Burke threw it through a rapid succession of sharp turns to avoid craters that suddenly gaped in front of them, proved no problem for the stabiliser holding the 30mm Rarden on target. Libby got off another clip as the last shell from the flak tank scooped a gob of metal from an angle of the roof, before exploding with an eardrum punishing roar on the side of the turret.

At the moment he mentally predicted, and at precisely the correct range, Libby saw on his thermal imager the pinkish shimmer of a distant angular outline blossom into a tall column of chasing shades of bright red. A check through the day-sight confirmed that, seven hundred yards away, the edge of a small wood was being brilliantly lit by a rising shower of incandescence, as the Russian vehicle's ammunition burned in spectacular fashion.

"It's just there, at the side of the road, by the burning tree." Hyde backed off the periscope and let Revell look.

"I knew this was going to be a shitty job." Dooley smacked a large fist into a dirty palm, as he and Cohen waited to hear what had happened to the other skimmer. "Is it a direct hit, Major?"

"Pretty close. There's a hell of a big hole in the road, right under their front end." The other carrier lay a good three hundred yards back along the road. It was prominently lit by the fires among the branches of the tall tree, and stood in the middle of a tract of featureless land that didn't offer a scrap of cover. There was the possibility that it was under enemy observation already. Taking the Iron Cow back there could kill them all.

"There's no sign of movement." It was at moments like this that Revell felt the full weight of command responsibility.

"Two or three men might make it safely on foot, just to check it out." Hyde realised what was going through the officer's head, and offered an alternative.

"We'll send two." The choice as to which two took Revell only a moment. "Dooley and Clarence, off you go. And move. I don't want to be hanging about here for long."

The flames from the distant houses threw long tongues of light and shadow across the fields, and the road stood out as a curling grey ribbon against the mixed and shifting shades of the farmland.

Hugging the hedgerow, the pair worked their way towards the stricken vehicle. The erratic circle of light from the guttering flames in the oak showed it standing just the other side of a wide steaming crater. One of the engine pods had been ripped off and whirled away by the blast.

"Christ, it's taken a belting." As they drew nearer, Dooley could see where the near miss by the powerful missile had shattered the vehicle's front as far back as the commander's cupola. The ride-skirts had been slashed and holed by fragments, and a couple of panels had gone altogether. There was a strong smell of kerosene, and hydraulic fluid spurted from a distorted ram attached to what was left of the ramp.

Smoke was curling from beneath the hull as Clarence crouched and kept watch, while Dooley tackled the buckled metal barring entrance to the crew compartment. Above them the breeze fanned sparks from the burning tree. With a loud creaking and rending the warped panel suddenly ceased its resistance.

The floor was slippery, and the passengers lay locked together in a tangle of arms and legs. Dooley tugged at a limb and someone groaned. "Give me a hand."

Together they hauled out a tall black. He was covered in blood from a mass of cuts, but apart from being dazed appeared to have no other injuries. They sat him at the crater's edge, where he rapidly began to recover, and went back in to investigate another source of groaning, nearer the back.

Several of the passengers had been decapitated by the scything hunks of metal that had come in through the front. A head rolled under Clarence's foot as he climbed over the heaped bodies to reach the other survivor. He had to grit his teeth and close his mind to what it was he was clambering over. He hated any form of physical contact, loathed the feel of other flesh on his. Even a handshake was more than he could abide. The proximity of others when travelling in the skimmer was something he'd forced himself to tolerate, but only because it served his purpose. He regarded it as a battle taxi; it took him to the killing ground so he put up with the crowding and jostling and smell. But it took a great effort for him to touch the still warm bodies, slippery and stinking of blood and vomit and half-digested food spilled from opened stomachs.

The second survivor was in a bad way, with an ugly gaping wound in the side of his head that their largest field dressing couldn't completely cover. Leaving him with the black, they returned for a last check.

Clarence stood and concentrated. "Do you hear something?"

He listened, but all Dooley could hear was the tree crackling outside, and an occasional ticking from the remaining engine as it cooled. "Let's get out, this can is brewing up."

As he went to leave, Dooley stopped abruptly and looked at a tangle of wire and distorted metalwork. He reached in and pulled a couple of loose sheets of aluminum aside. "It's the sarge!"

Master Sergeant Windle was still alive. He had fallen from the commander's seat and been almost completely hidden by the mass of metal that the external explosion had forced back and wrapped around him. His injuries were terrible, but he retained a measure of consciousness and limply gestured with his remaining hand to Dooley.

Even uniting their efforts, there was no way Clarence and the big man could free the sergeant from the tangled metal. Smoke was filtering into the compartment, and the pool of blood on the hull floor was beginning to boil. The stink of burning rubber now swamped all other smells.

A gaping wound in his throat had deprived the sergeant of speech, but he pointed repeatedly to Dooley's slung Colt Commando submachine gun and then to himself. His meaning was abundantly clear. Understanding that he was trapped, and aware that the craft was burning, he didn't want to be still alive when the flames reached him.

"Shit, I can't do that. What the hell does he want to go getting himself into a mess like this for?" Dooley half-raised the short-barrelled version of the M16, then lowered it again.

"It's that or leave him to burn. We've still got to get the other two back to the Cow." Clarence looked at his watch. They'd already been gone too long. "What are you going to do?"

"Oh Jesus. Killing him would be like killing our luck." The Colt was heavy in Dooley's hands, its metal and plastic wet with the sweat of his palms. He looked at Clarence, sensing that the sergeant's eyes were still on him.

"You want me to do it?"

Small spurts of red flame came from an electronics panel at the back, adding further urgency. Dooley snatched up a .45 automatic from the floor and tried to fit it into Windle's hand, moulding the stained fingers around it. The moment he let go, it fell from the nerveless grasp and clattered back to the floor.

"Yeah, yeah you do it." The big man stepped aside.

Clarence borrowed Dooley's submachine gun, refraining from using his own rifle for a task such as this. He pushed the tip of the flash suppressor to within an inch of the dying man's open mouth, and fired. The noise in the small metal compartment was painful. As the back of his head flew off, Windle's body arched forward in a spasm. The dead man's teeth clamped hard on the barrel as the muscles of his jaw locked.

At the moment of firing Dooley was already going out, now he looked back to see the sniper struggling to extract the weapon from the face of the corpse.

"Come on, it's burning."

"Do you damn well think I don't know that. Your blasted sergeant won't let go."

Acrid smoke from burning wiring filled the skimmer with fumes that made breathing difficult. A section of the floor was taking on a wrinkled semi-molten look. Grey brain matter boiled like foam in a never ending stream from the eyes of a severed head.

Hurrying back in, Dooley put his foot on the dead sergeant's face and, as Clarence wrenched the weapon back and forth, teeth snapped and splintered and it was suddenly free.

Pushing one and carrying the other survivor they raced back to their transport. Even as Dooley, last to board, was stepping on to the ramp the craft lifted and they were under way again.

"Rinehart, you're a lucky shit." Abe Cohen kept saying it as he watched Hyde binding two field dressings arranged side by side to cover the gaping hole in Nelson's head. "When a clean-living boy like that gets hit, and even old Windle buys it, how come a bum like you sails through with only a few scratches? Hell, this shitty war is all mixed up."

"Must be on account of my fine and wholesome nature. I guess God is just smiling down on one of his favourite children."

Dooley leant across and leered into the black's broad features. "Oh yeah, then how come you had treatment

47

for a dose of the pox last year. Tell me, Jango, where does that fit in with 'wholesome'?"

"That's a damned lie. I ain't used that weapon in such a long time I don't reckon it could fire any more." His leer matched Dooley's.

"Let's have some quiet in here. This is Indian country, we could run into trouble anytime."

"Hey, Major, that weren't no boy scout troop we tangled with back there."

Dooley was ignored. Officer and sergeant were busy conferring over a large scale map.

"We should be able to cross the river here." With his little finger Hyde indicated a spot seven miles down stream from Gifhorn. "If we do it there we avoid having to cross the Oker as well. If we travel parallel with the bank, once we're over it'll bring us to the camp."

"OK everybody." Revell reached for his 12 gauge assault rifle. "I want you all on your toes. We'll be slowing for a river crossing in about ten minutes. I'm hoping we can make it without trouble but . . ."

The skimmer shuddered and lurched sideways under the impact of a massive blow. As the lights went out, the last thing Collins saw was Corporal Howard arching back from the radar console with a huge hole in his chest.

Chapter Four

"Shut your bloody noise. Shut up." Hyde's voice boomed out of the darkness.

The confused babble of curses and shouts that had filled the compartment the instant after impact ceased, but Revell still had to shout to make himself heard above the crash and clatter of loosened panels and external stores, when he realised the internal communications system had failed.

"Keep moving, into those woods dead ahead. Get us in there."

Intermittent showers of sparks from exposed wiring in the ruins of the scanner console provided the only illumination. By the erratic light Burke could be seen fighting to keep the skimmer on course. The smooth ride was gone, the craft dipped continually to one side and bucked at every minor undulation. All of Burke's skills couldn't prevent the Iron Cow travelling with a peculiar crab-like motion.

"The buggers have taken off some of the ride-skirt. We can't go far like this."

Saplings began to snap before them as they plunged into the woods. Others, more pliant, scraped noisily under the buoyancy tanks beneath the cabin of the rushing vehicle, to whiplash back to an upright position after its passing.

Another high velocity tungsten-tipped round zipped past, losing fractions of its armour-defeating speed with every bough it sheered and trunk it clipped.

Blue flame showed briefly among the spark-lit innards of the radar console, before Cohen at last managed to score a direct hit with a well directed squirt from a fire-extinguisher.

The continuous minor collisions stopped as the craft slewed across a rutted track, and then its front dipped violently as it nosed over the edge of a steep decline. Turbofans screaming in reverse, the skimmer slithered down out of control. There was a succession of heavy bruising impacts and jumps as the vehicle defeated and ran over several large trees, throwing the men about; then a cascade of hail-like sounds as masses of stones and gravel pummelled the metal hull. A final jarring collision that brought Libby tumbling down out of his turret and the Iron Cow came to rest.

Revell lunged forward to prevent Burke from reversing them off whatever it was that had at last arrested their mad career. "Let's see where we are first."

The driver's screen was still working, but with its limited field of vision revealed nothing but a section of steeply rising bank immediately in front of them. It was liberally dotted with substantial trees whose gnarled exposed roots bound the mossy slope together. The view he obtained using the all round infra-red facility in the turret was more informative.

They had come to rest in a shallow stream bed, against the still massive remains of a storm-toppled elm, at the bottom of a steep-sided ravine. Behind them, a number of uprooted trees marked their descent.

Using the periscopes, Hyde had been carrying out a similar inspection. "Looks like as good a place as any, Major, to stop and see what the damage is."

"I agree. Post two men with the MG at the top of the slope behind us, where they can keep a watch on that track. Then I want a damage report, and fast."

The beam of a torch flickered across Corporal Howard's ruined torso to his white, blood-flecked death mask. His body still lay where it had originally come to rest, wedged between the ammunition boxes and a bench. For a while the light hovered about the wide-eyed face, then moved on as Hyde turned to the holed scanner board.

"He was our only electronics man. Burke's OK with engines, and Libby knows the hardware of any weapons system, but circuits and silicon chips . . ." Hyde shook his head.

"Cohen . . ." Revell didn't get to finish the sentence.

"I'll get on it right away, Major, but I can't promise a lot. Shit," another pencil line of light flickered on as Cohen sat in the operator's seat. "This looks like an MBT has been driven through it. I think maybe a heartfelt prayer would be as useful as a soldering iron."

Cool clean air flushed the interior clear of smoke and stench as Libby and Collins went out. They splashed through the ankle-deep water and then immediately tackled the steep slope.

Encumbered as he was by six one-hundred-round

51

belts of ammunition, as well as his own rifle and a satchel of grenades, plus a spare barrel for the machine gun, Collins was trailing by some yards before they were out of sight of the skimmer.

While Dooley and Rinehart set about extricating Howard's body from its awkward resting place, the others began the inspection of their transport. The lists of damage suffered became steadily longer.

Hyde's finger tapped the edge of the large irregular hole below the port engine pod. "Looks like it was deflected when it hit the engine-mounting bracket. The shell went down and ripped the skirt panels off, the bracket went through here travelling upwards at about forty-five degrees, penetrated the inner hull and went straight through the guts of Howard's scanner."

"And then straight through Howard's guts."

"Shut up, Burke." Hyde stood up. "We can replace the damaged and missing skirt panels, but there's nothing we can do about the engine mounting. It's not just that we don't carry any, the studs were snapped off, it'll be a workshop job."

"She'll still motor alright though?" Looking closely, Revell could see bright unpainted metal where the bracket had been ripped away.

Hyde let Burke answer.

"Might be a bit more vibration, and if we start clouting a load more trees then I can't say how long the other four will hold, but she'll motor. I'd prefer not to go above fifty though, if it can be avoided. If it does break loose it'll tip us over and we'll burn for sure."

"How about you, Cohen, what's your news?" It was

only because he could see the unnaturally humped shoulder line, the distinctive silhouette of a flak jacket, that Revell could identify who was on the ramp. The darkness beneath the overhanging foliage of the trees was almost total.

"Some good, some bad, Major. You could say our eyes are gone but our ears are still working. We've lost all visual systems except the turret and cupola infrared, and the driver's image intensifier. But if I rig up what's left of the hostile fire locator and active radar detector so they'll give an audio signal instead, we'll still know when someone is looking at us, or chucking shit in our direction. We just won't know where from and how much, but it'll be better than nothing."

"How long will it take?" Sparks trailed behind the red dot of the major's cigarette butt as he flicked it away. It died with a faint hiss among the damp stones at the water's edge.

"If someone holds the torch for me, and provided I don't run into any fresh problems, an hour. It won't be pretty, but it'll work. Only someone of my genius could do it, it ain't exactly a standard conversion."

"Save the patting yourself on the back for when you've made it work. OK, you can have Rinehart."

The major bent down, cupped his hands under the surface of the shallow water and splashed his face. He dried himself on the sleeve of his camouflage jacket. "How long 'til dawn, Sergeant."

"Two hours. Are we still trying to make it tonight, Major?"

"Can we get to safe ground in the time we'll have left after Cohen has fixed the board?"

"If we don't run into any more problems, yes. But

53

there won't be any margin for error."

"Then we're still trying to make it tonight." Revell looked up at the invisible umbrella of leaves eighty feet above their heads. "That won't give us any cover from multi-spectral reconnaissance if the Reds send over sky-spies, and there's a chance they will after tonight. Our best bet is to be far away when they get round to looking."

A match flared beside them as Burke lit a cigarette.

"What the hell are you still standing about for?" Hyde turned on him. "Get those spare skirt panels off the roof. Are you waiting for me to bloody do it for you?"

"On me own? By me self? Those things weigh a ton."

"Seventy-nine pounds each," Sergeant Hyde corrected.

"And what about the water? I'll catch me death of cold."

"You'll catch something in a minute."

Revell was just going back into the skimmer, and heard the exchange. "He can have Dooley to help him, Sergeant Hyde."

The big man came splashing through the water muttering obscenities. "I was just going to have a crap. Why didn't you lot keep your mouths shut till I'd finished?"

"Because at the moment I don't want the stream dammed. Now stop the backchat and get on with it."

"Do you think you can make me if I don't want to?" Dooley straightened up to his full six-foot-four and towered over the sergeant.

Burke's voice floated down from above. "If you want to start chucking weight about, give me a hand. I'm fucking rupturing meself up here."

Dooley didn't look up. When he turned away from the sergeant to unfasten a tool locker, out of the corner of his eye he saw Burke standing on the skimmer's roof with two of the heavy metal-bound skirt panels held high above his head.

"That's enough arsing about. Fetch that stuff down here on the double and do the ruddy job." As Hyde turned to leave, there was a huge splash behind him and a fan of water hit his back and showered past on either side.

"Sorry, Sarge, it slipped."

Although, being much closer to the point of impact, Dooley must have been absolutely soaked by the "accident", Hyde could hear him fighting to suppress a laugh, and mostly failing. He gritted his teeth, took a deep breath and kept going. There would be other times, if the Ruskies didn't get them first, when he would be able to get those two back into line, and he'd enjoy doing it.

In order to keep the Iron Cow's IR signature as low as possible, they had removed to a flood-scooped hollow beneath the overhanging roots of a beech for a brew.

Nelson had been double dosed and left on board. There was nothing else they could do for him. The terrible nerve-jangling hooting he'd made for all of ten minutes had forced them to administer the second injection. Now, for a while, he had lapsed into oblivion.

Sergeant Hyde found an early opportunity to extract some measure of revenge on Dooley and Burke, when he sent them to relieve the two men on guard at the top of the ravine, only a minute after they'd finished bolting on the replacement skirts.

Begrudgingly, causing the maximum disruption, the pair extracted themselves from where, by dint of much wriggling and removing of pebbles from beneath their backsides, they'd managed to attain a degree of comfort and left the hollow.

As they did, the tops of the trees were thrown into violent motion. Both men hurled themselves flat as with a loud whirring of blades a helicopter flew over. The trees continued to thrash back and forth and shower down leaves for some time after the chopper had gone.

Before the trees had settled down the pair were up and running for the slope.

"Bloody hell. From the racket you two were making I thought a bleeding elephant was coming up behind us. You made more noise than that chopper."

"Piss off and get your coffee." Dooley began to hack at the sides of the shallow excavation to accommodate his larger frame.

Unable to resist it, Libby offered a parting shot. "You'll find the worms quite friendly. Have a nice stay."

Burke threw a shovelful of dirt after the departing pair. "You reckon that chopper spotted us?"

"How the fuck should I know? Probably wasn't even on a recon' flight, just on his way home. Mind you, if he were taking a few frames he'll be in for a surprise. He'll have one of a pair of silly fuckers laying face down in the stream. That'll keep the unimaginative bastards guessing, they'll wonder what sort of silly-arse games we're playing now." Pushing one final spadeful of soil aside, Dooley settled down.

"You're fucking mad." Burke couldn't decide if the American was serious or not.

"The whole fucking world is mad, or we wouldn't be here. But it is, and we are; so let's enjoy it."

Still undecided, Burke thought he might as well join in. "You're right. The weather's nice, we're in the country and soon the little birdies will be singing . . ."

"And right now I'm going for a little crappies." Wandering off a few paces into the middle of the track, Dooley began to lower his pants.

". . . and we're about to witness yet another demonstration of nature's own little miracle." Burke plucked a small white daisy from the midst of a tuft of coarse leaves. "How to convert a pound and a half of steaming hot shit into a gem of miniature perfection."

"Fuck off. This ain't no fertiliser I'm dropping. What happens when you put your foot in some really pig-shit awful dog dirt?"

"I stop, feel ill and don't wear the shoes again for ages."

"Exactly. Well, my crap has much the same effect on tanks and their crews. In the right place at the right time, with the right amount of Ex-Lax, I could stop a bloody regiment of T84s."

To take his mind off the revolting sights and sounds emanating from a few yards away, Burke began to systematically take the flower apart, having to squint to see it at all. "He loves me, he loves me not, he loves me, he loves . . ."

"Will that old crate of ours get us there?" Collins blew

on the boiling hot coffee, and passed it rapidly back and forth from hand to hand.

"It'll get us there." Clarence drank his mugful scalding hot. It was his theory that at that temperature you couldn't taste how awful it was. "I must admit I am more concerned that it should be able to get us back."

"She'll make it, there and back." Like the others Hyde kept quiet for a moment to catch the argument between Cohen and Rinehart that floated to them from the vehicle.

Cohen's criticism was indistinct, but Rinehart's reply was clear enough.

"And if you don't like the way I hold this torch, then you can tie it to your fancy shaped pisser and do the job on your own."

"How come they didn't just stick us in a chopper, buzz over and drop us right on the target? We'd be there and back inside two hours." Collins blew on his coffee.

"Because war is an art." Clarence took the answer upon himself. "And NATO creative ability does not yet stretch to finding a way to let fixed or rotary wing aircraft survive for more than, what? one and a half minutes? in enemy air space. I am all for experimentation, but not when it includes the near certainty of whirling down from a thousand feet in a burning and disintegrating helicopter."

"Balls."

"Have you finished, Rinehart?"

"All finished, Major. I think our little friend is intoning a prayer over it now, he kinda uses God like an electronics troubleshooter."

"What did you mean by balls?" Clarence steered the

conversation back to the previous subject.

"What I said, balls. There's no damned art in war. Where's the art in super-napalm, or suitcase-sized nukes, or dumdums. What you said is a load of bullshit."

"I didn't use art in that sense, you ignorant . . ."

"That's enough." The humour had gone out of the exchange. Revell had caught the sudden edge in Clarence's voice, and it made the back of his neck prickle. For all the man's quiet manner and well educated tones, there was something very deep, very dangerous, in the sniper.

"I got this feeling. Like it just ain't going to be a good day." Through one of the rare gaps in the interwoven branches high above them, Rinehart watched a tiny streamer of red flame being towed across the sky, betraying the path of an aircraft in trouble.

"I know what you mean." Libby poured himself another coffee. "I've found that when things are really bad, they have a habit of getting worse."

The flame-tail was suddenly tipped with a flaring ball of yellow and white that expanded rapidly, and then faded just as swiftly. The aircraft crew's trouble had just become infinitely worse.

Chapter Five

The definition of the image intensifier had not been improved by the pounding the vehicle's electrics had taken, and Burke had to call on all his skills as they followed the stone and tree-trunk strewn course of the stream. In places the water had cut a narrow winding channel between almost perpendicular banks. Had the precipitate descent of the preceding hour been at one of those spots, none of them would have survived.

"We're coming out into the open now." The skimmer slowed to a crawl as Burke nosed it from the last of the cover. On the major's instructions he now swung the Iron Cow up out of the gravel bed of the stream and on to the lush meadowland that flanked it.

"At least there's no reception committee waiting for us." Revell slowly rotated the cupola to check the flat land about them. "Right, slow ahead. At this stage I think silence might offer us a better defence than speed. Stop on the river bank when we reach it."

The turbines sent a shiver through the craft as they slowed. Burke alternately lowered and increased the rpm, searching for a power band that would stress the overtaxed engine mounts as little as possible.

A wide shining strip suddenly showed on the driver's screen. The hovercraft flattened another hundred yards of the tall grasses, and then the noise of the engines fell away to a whisper as it coasted to a stop and settled beneath the dangling tips of a willow.

"What the hell have we stopped for? Let's get across." Dooley used one of the periscopes set in the roof to peer out at the pale expanse of the river Aller, stretching away to right and left before them.

He was completely ignored by Hyde and Revell as they compared the view from the cupola with their map. Carpet bombing of the far bank had breached it, allowing the river to flood beyond its normal confines and increase its width by spreading into the neglected fields.

"Most of the landmarks have gone, and the rest of the landscape has been so knocked about it's hardly recognisable." The sergeant snatched another look through a periscope, then studied the view on Burke's screen.

"Take your time. I'd rather you were sure." The pencil Revell was holding tapped a random morse code on a corner of the map board.

Although the words didn't say it, Hyde sensed the impatience underlying them. He climbed up for another look. There was something, about a thousand yards off, the ruins of a building. It was in the correct place, but the outline wasn't how he remembered it. If it was the old processing plant then the roof and both silos and chimneys were missing. Other components of his field of vision looked vaguely familiar. A pile of rubble where a large house had been, leaning stumps where a copse of tall oaks had stood. Damn those bombers. Sod it, it felt right, it must be . . .

"Yes, this is about it. We're closer than I thought, but our detour accounts for that. We'll cross here, and then it's only a couple of miles to a place where we can leave the Cow in safety while we find the workshops. That's if the airforce have stuck to the rules and not bombed closer to the camp than they're supposed to."

Cautiously Burke eased the machine forward until it overhung the six-foot drop to the sluggishly flowing water. A shouted warning, and then he nudged it a fraction further and the skimmer swung down. A curtain of spray rose up as the leading edge of the skirt and hull dipped into the Aller, and air being thrust out by the turbofans fought to keep the craft on an even keel. There was another towering cascade as the rear of the hovercraft pancaked down and stabilised the machine.

Spray clouds surrounded and followed them across the river and again in the swamp-like fields beyond.

"How is he?" Collins leant across to where Rinehart was trying to resecure the bulky dressing that ineffectually bound Nelson's gaping wound.

"Pretty bad. Can't see him hanging on long unless we can get him fixed up proper, real soon."

The bandage slipped, and as it fell from the wound it was followed by a gush of blood that brought with it shards of bone and blobs of spongy white matter.

"Here, hold this." Rinehart pushed the sterile dressing back in place and while Collins held it with eyes averted, bound it to the wounded soldier's head with many intricate windings of crêpe. "He's gonna wake up again soon, and when he does he's gonna make an awful noise."

"What we could do with is a nice big-boned nurse, all starch and black stockings, with a juicy fat arse and nutcracker thighs." Dooley made crude appreciative noises by smacking his lips together.

"Don't forget the tits." Having overheard, Burke joined in. "Don't forget the tits."

"Never do. That's why I like bending them over and taking them from behind. That way you get plenty of good handfuls as well. You can't do it from the front, least I can't, they always tell me to use me elbows 'cause I'm too heavy." The big man grinned at Collins. "How about you, kid, how do you like them? Had any tasty schoolgirls lately? Or aren't you old enough for them yet?"

"Shut up, you poisonous lout."

In the noise of the compartment Clarence's words weren't clear and it was a few seconds before their meaning sunk in and wiped the leer off Dooley's face. A ham-sized fist rocketed towards the sniper.

Clarence didn't move until the last possible instant before the huge paw would have struck him, then he half-turned in his seat as the dirty knuckles swept past his chin with only a fraction of an inch to spare, and brought up his rifle from between his knees, driving the tip of the barrel into Dooley's forearm. It sank past the sight into the thick flesh.

Dooley bellowed as the pain made his fist spring open. He held his arm and examined the livid bruise that was fast spreading on it. "What sort of fucking trick is that?" There was an agonising sensation of intense pins-and-needles in the limb, and he couldn't move his fingers. "Feels like you've fucking broken it."

"It isn't, you'll recover." Taking a clean, neatly folded tissue from his breast pocket, Clarence wiped and scrubbed his rifle. He kept on long after any trace of the big man's sweat had been removed by the short, brusque actions.

"Neat, very neat. You've got good reflexes there, man." Rinehart had watched with amazement and admiration.

Though he waited for some acknowledgement of the compliment, none was forthcoming. "You'll have to forgive old Dooley here. He's really a no-holds-barred man, he don't usually go in for such refinements as punching."

"He'll find out." Flexing his hand as a degree of feeling returned to it, Dooley didn't look up as he spoke.

"Save it for the Commies." Revell had been about to intervene when Dooley made his move, but he'd seen the look in the Britisher's pale unblinking eyes and instinctively known that he didn't have to. If the big man had been more observant, he too might have held off and saved himself a deal of pain. But maybe not— Dooley was the sort who always had to learn lessons the hard way.

Hyde hadn't even bothered to watch what was going on, let alone get involved.

"You don't bother much about your men, Sergeant."

"I don't have to, Major. They get in and out of trouble quite well enough on their own. If it's minor stuff, I let them get on with it."

65

Revell was finding it difficult to fathom the British squad. They were an unlikely mixture. A lonely kid, a near psychotic sniper, a brilliant combat driver who could tire himself just by breathing, an efficient turret gunner who was frighteningly normal by comparison and a horrifically mutilated sergeant whose principal control over his men was his total confidence in them, and their trust in him.

Combined with the individuals Revell still had left out of his command, it was a weird assortment of types and talents, but maybe just because of that it had the markings of one hell of a good team, so long as it could learn to work like one.

"Just two miles from the refugee camp now, Major." The sky was beginning to lighten, and Hyde couldn't decide which was best, normal optics or the various imaging systems available to him. "The Russians have a dawn-to-dusk curfew on the place, so that still gives us twenty minutes before the first of the mobs will be leaving the shelters on foraging trips. Then they swarm all over the area, scavenging for anything they can find."

"Where's this place we can hide up? It'll have to be good."

"Isn't it just." Burke's words lacked enthusiasm.

"You just drive."

"Sod it, Sarge, isn't there anywhere else?"

"No, it's dead ahead now. Take us in very slow and don't put us down till I tell you."

Burke brought the skimmer's speed down to a crawl. "You've got to be fucking joking. Did you think I would?"

The Iron Cow began to climb a gentle slope towards the dense dark wall of trees at the perimeter of an area of woodland. Very carefully, Burke piloted the hovercraft between two well-weathered stakes. Barbed wire grated beneath the belly of the machine and then the noise was gone and the tangled mass of undergrowth engulfed them.

Several times, despite the intense care he took, their driver couldn't prevent the skimmer from nudging trees it had to squeeze past. Angular dark shapes, tantalisingly indistinct, were glimpsed at the edge of the screen as they drove in deeper. Sergeant Hyde stood behind the driver's seat, scrutinising every inch of the woods and signalling slight corrections of course by tapping Burke's left or right shoulder.

"Forward a little more, left, left; a little more. Steady. Put her down."

The engine note remained the same. Burke made no move to follow the last instruction, maintaining the same ride height.

"I said put us down."

Their driver still made no move to comply, finely balancing the controls to keep them hovering in the same spot.

"Do as the sergeant says." Revell added his weight.

"You do know where we are, don't you, Major?" With a slight movement of the left steering pedal Burke corrected a tendency on the part of the machine to drift to the right. "This is a bloody minefield. The place is stiff with the ruddy things. Those are wrecks out there." He pointed at the screen, to a vague squat outline some yards ahead of them.

Revell looked at Hyde. There was nothing in the man's face to give him any clues, there was hardly any face, but the sergeant's manner didn't suggest he was contemplating suicide and intent on taking them all with him. "So put us down gently."

For a couple of seconds Burke still stubbornly resisted, then began very gradually to reduce engine power to enable the craft to settle. All the time he made minute adjustments to keep the position Hyde had indicated.

Like all of the others Rinehart held his breath until the Iron Cow was safely grounded, then let it out in a sigh of relief. "What do you want us to do now, Sarge. Go for a stroll through the woods?"

"This is the only place the refugees don't come foraging for metal. They're like a load of jackdaws, pinch anything . . ."

"Hey, Dooley, you got a load of relatives around here some place?" It was Cohen who interrupted the British NCO.

". . . that's the reason the Commies don't lace this area with ground radar surveillance dishes. They'd all be turned into frying pans by the end of the day. About the only things the refugees won't go near is mines. These derelicts have been here two years and they haven't been touched in all that time."

"How well do you know this camp, Sergeant?" Revell got in first, before Dooley could take up Cohen on his remark.

"Pretty well, I expect it's changed shape a bit since the last time I was here, about four months ago, but the Reds don't like them to get above a hundred thousand so overall it'll be much the same. Certainly the inner areas will be. It's the later additions, the most recently tacked on shelters that alter the appearance and can get you lost."

"At that size it's going to be too big to scout on foot, even if we weren't spotted as we roamed about. Do you have any contacts in there, who might be helpful with the right persuasion?"

He'd have to answer carefully, Hyde was fully aware of that. Both sides, in theory at least, enforced the Red Cross's rules about no military interference in the camps beyond minimum policing; but Soviet commanders broke them when it suited them, and few soldiers on either side could resist the obvious attractions of the various "entertainments" the camps offered. Many NATO troops made a point of carrying extra rations and similar temptations that could be exchanged for the frequently desperate refugees' gold, or jewellery, or bodies. He didn't know the major's standpoint on the matter so he played safe, he wasn't about to lose his stripes or get himself slung out of the army, just because he spoke without thinking.

"I've heard of a couple of places where we might get information about any new activities the Reds have started in the area. I expect I can find them."

"Don't be cute, Sergeant Hyde. I know what goes on in the camps, I'm not trying to catch you out. Considering the mayhem we hope to let loose before the day is out, bending a few rules isn't going to bother me. Now, yes or no?"

"I'll give it an hour. My best cover will be to mix and merge with the civvies. Better break out the rags, Collins."

From a locker Collins dragged out a kitbag, and started to extract various articles of patched and faded clothing.

"Fuck that." Dooley moved away. "I kept thinking someone had wind. It weren't, it were those, phew." He held his nose.

Clarence toed a garment that was dropped. "If you go into the camps you not only have to look right, you have to smell right. You should feel completely at home."

"Don't aggravate him, Clarence. You know he's got a temper worse than yours." From the heap Hyde picked a large soiled windcheater. "Scruffy so it won't draw attention, bulky enough to hide a weapon. Soap doesn't figure anywhere on the list of priority supplies the Red Cross and Oxfam bring in, so it's no good walking about with a well scrubbed look smelling of bloody violets." He pulled on an oversized pair of Levi cords.

"You can pick me an outfit too, Sergeant. I want to see the ground for myself; and we'll take one other man, your choice."

About to secure the top of the jeans with a grubby polka-dot necktie improvised as a belt, Hyde paused. "That's not a good idea, Major. The civvies won't give us away if they spot us; the Ruskies never pay for information and in the camps everyone wants to be anonymous, not draw attention to themselves. But if they heard your accent . . . Well, they'd be down on us like a swarm of locusts and the Reds will spot a riot a mile away."

70

"You saying we ain't popular?" Dooley stuck his chin out in an aggressive fashion.

"That's just the point, you're too damned popular. It's been just us British, and the West Germans, in this sector for the whole of the war so far. We're not exactly overburdened with luxuries to give away or barter, but the refugees think you lot are loaded with goodies. They'll tear you apart looking for them."

"I'm still going, Sergeant. Pick our third man."

Hyde knew before he looked round which of his own men would have his eyes locked on him. Sure enough it was Libby. Their turret gunner had ducked down from his perch and was sidling towards the old clothes. So why not? He had more experience than Collins, was more useful than Burke and more predictable than Clarence. And if he had a special reason for spending as much time as he could in the camps, what the hell, he didn't let it interfere with his work.

With a slight inclination of his head Libby returned the nod that Hyde made to him.

"Shit, why him, Major. What's wrong with one of us, ain't we good enough all of a sudden? You want I should make a list of our good points?" Cohen's protest was noisy.

"Sure, if you've got ten seconds to spare. When you've finished you can do something useful. Open every hatch and port. I want this machine cooled right down. I don't want it standing out like a come-and-get-us neon sign on the IR scanner of any Ruskie sky-spy."

After a cursory inspection Revell put on the much repaired and ill-matched suit jacket and baggy worsted trousers he was handed. From their state he'd half

71

expected them to be crawling, but they weren't. After hitching the various components of the outfit closer about him, and fastening it together as best he could with a selection of rusty safety pins Hyde provided, he was satisfied that it adequately concealed the .45 automatic and grenades he carried.

This was the first time Revell had been into one of the big camps. In the Balkans the refugees had been scattered in thousands of tiny settlements, kept that way by the Yugoslav partisans despite the Communists' efforts to the contrary, not herded together into carefully defined and controlled localities as they were here in the north.

The only advantage Revell could see in the "bigger is better" policy, apart from the easing of distribution problems for the paltry amount of aid the relief agencies brought in, was the creation of large tracts of land that could be declared free-fire zones which particularly suited the Russian style of warfare. The only benefit to the NATO forces was that it released every gunner and bomb-aimer from the constraints imposed by the fear of unleashing barrages of bombs on to innocent heads.

Innocent heads. How easy the trite tailored phrases of the propaganda machine popped into his thoughts. There weren't many innocents left among the refugees now, not after two years. Those who hadn't been prepared to grab and cheat and lie and steal were gone: into mass graves, on to communal pyres. Those who were left were hardened by twenty-four months of deprivation, sharpened by the same length of time spent living by their wits. They could be as dangerous as the enemy to the unwary, the inexperienced, the soft-hearted. Revell had seen one of his own men die, trampled to death under the crush of women and children to whom he'd been trying to distribute spare rations.

That was what happened if you let the Zone get to you. He wasn't about to let it happen to him, couldn't afford to if he wanted to stay alive.

NATO Intelligence Report. 887/G2/57756 GRADE 'A'
For distribution to all Planning Staffs

The Soviet 97th Technical Support Battalion has now been positively identified in the northern sector of the Zone. Limited satellite surveillance time for this theatre has prevented precise location, but evidence indicates that the 97th have established a workshop among, or close to the refugee settlements near Gifhorn on the east bank of the river Aller, opposite the Hanover salient.

It is likely that the 97th is now engaged in a major re-fit and up-dating programme on the armoured vehicles of the Soviet 2nd Guards Army.

Under Major I. V. Pakilev the 97th has come to be regarded by the Russian High Command as their finest Field Workshop Unit. It has been featured on several occasions in Pravda, and in both national and international propaganda.

The destruction of this unit would be a severe blow to the 2nd Guards Army's preparations for its next offensive against the salient, anticipated in late August, early September. Its loss would also constitute a grave embarrassment to the Soviet High Command.

Chapter Six

"What in fuck's name made him leave you in charge?"
As his booming voice filled the interior, Dooley dug
Cohen in the ribs with a finger made only marginally
less filthy than his others by its having been up his nose
a minute before.

Cohen completely ignored the sarcasm and physical
emphasis and went on with his work at the console.
He'd accepted the responsibility thrown to him by the
major's parting remark philosophically. So all of a ·
sudden he had a squad of his own, big deal. He hadn't
the stripes or the extra money to go with it, so what was
there to get excited about—nothing. All he could get
out of it was trouble. Now he didn't have just himself to
worry about, now he had this assortment of hard cases,
head cases and stretcher cases. That was a favour?
Favours like that he could do without. He had enough
work to do trying to lace together what was left of the
electronics, without playing nursemaid to punks and
deviants.

Failing to get their temporary section leader to rise

to his clumsy bait, Dooley sought other fish. He cast round and found Burke. "How'd your sergeant manage to barbecue himself like that, was he too slow backing off the heat and friction caused by you rushing about?"

"Could be." Burke stretched slowly, and when he'd finished went back to dreamily gazing at the banded green landscape on the driver's screen.

Though he wasn't achieving what he'd hoped, Dooley persisted. "Don't you do anything that might strain you, wouldn't like you to wear yourself out before your time."

"No danger, mate, no danger." Between yawns Burke looked at his watch, shook it, held it to his ear and then, finding his arm made an adequate pillow on the bulkhead, went to sleep.

"Give up, man. You ain't gonna get any of this crowd going, you'll have to work it off some other way."

"Piss off." Ignoring the black, Dooley tried willing the pain in his back to go away, it wouldn't. Shit, it was always the same. The doc had said it was just tension, fuck him, what did he know. There was only one way to ease it, beside going into action. Had they been anywhere but in the centre of a minefield he'd have gone out and smashed to pieces the first inanimate object he encountered. That had worked before. He couldn't do that here, instead he roughly barged to the front of the compartment, and stepped out on to the ramp.

Collins heard the massive roaring bellow, and shivered. Long ago he'd come to the conclusion that the world must be mad to permit such an insanely dangerous conflict; now he felt he was fighting it with

78

men who were dangerously insane.

The war had taken them all, and turned them inside out. It was as though every last human trait in them, whether for good or evil, was being forced to the fore as their only remaining defence against the totally dehumanising effect of the Zone.

As Dooley's shout was first caught then mercifully smothered by the dense trees, it occurred to Collins to wonder how long it would be before he became a shell, a husk, labelled only by extremes of mood as human. When Libby had been chosen to go with Hyde and Revell he'd thought himself lucky to be left behind. Now, as he watched Clarence's legs continually circling as he laboriously handcranked the turret round in a perpetual search of a target, he reconsidered.

The sun had been up an hour before the trio finally extricated themselves from the wooded graveyard of men and machines that hid their transport. Tracks that Hyde remembered had ceased to exist, reclaimed by the unchecked growth that also sought to conceal the wrecked and gutted remains of forty or more Russian armoured personnel carriers. Here and there, besides a trackless rusted bulk, the dull white bone dome of a fox-gnawed skull showed among the rank grass and weeds.

Close to the perimeter of the woods there was more recent evidence of violence. The rotting remains of bodies still bearing traces of civilian clothes lay inside the flimsy barricade that girded the lethal area.

There were already a few refugees about, some

79

working in small groups gleaning missed corners of fields for a few ears of half-ripened barley: others, in twos and threes, staggered along under the weight of ill-trimmed logs. It was like viewing the periphery of a bizarre human ants' nest, the object of whose workers was obscure and the result of whose labours were pathetic.

No one looked at the three men who trudged along the dusty well-worn path towards the camp, even though they passed quite close to some of the later risers.

The dress of most was as incongruous and ill matched as that of Revell and his companions. Among a group of middle-aged men squabbling and coming near to blows over a wormy sugar-beet, one wore a tattered raincoat over shorts and rollneck jumper, another sported a paint-daubed pair of overalls and golf cap and a third, shoeless and carrying a rolled-up plastic cycle cape, had on a filthy T-shirt and the bottom portion of what might once have been an expensive tweed suit, a lady's judging by the way the trousers fastened.

"Almost there. It's just over the next rise." For the last five minutes Hyde had been scanning the sky ahead, and now he saw it, the thin grey threads of smoke from countless numbers of meagre cooking fires. They rose up to blend together to form a dirty veil in the cloudless sky.

Now there were more people about, and a few of the shuffling figures threw curious glances at the three men who walked against the predominant flow of traffic away from the camp. Not many, though, after a glance at the sergeant's gross disfigurement looked longer, or a second time.

They paused beside a hedge as a Russian Hind helicopter gunship lazily beat its way across the area at two thousand feet, and on out of sight into the thickening smoke haze over the camp.

"Do the Reds take an interest in the camps?" Revell felt less conspicuous when they started walking again, they'd been the only ones to stop.

"Sometimes. A lot of Commie deserters find their way there, and usually end up banding together in a gang. After a while they get cocky and try raiding Ruskie supply dumps, then they get jumped on. The Reds move in, there's a couple of days excitement, a few refugees get clobbered in the crossfire and then everything settles down again. Usually though they're just content to keep an eye on the agency people, and maybe work a few foot patrols, plus of course they jam every frequency to stop news getting in or out. Normally in the five-mile so-called civilian area around a camp they keep out of sight, when it suits them."

"There's the camp, Sarge." It looked bigger than Libby remembered it, had sprawled out across a few more hills. A straggling line of tiled rooftops and the jutting spire of a church marked at its centre the little village around which it had so explosively grown. Through a tear in the old coat he wore Libby put his hand into a pocket of his jacket. His fingers sought the familiar shape and feel of the small square of plastic covered photograph and his hand closed about it. Perhaps this time . . .

"Where the hell do we start?" They stood on ground

81

a little higher than the camp, but even from that vantage point Revell could make out no pattern or system in the layout of the close-spaced huts and ramshackle shelters. Here and there a short stretch of path might be seen, but within a couple of yards it was lost to sight as it dog-legged around another of the randomly situated hovels.

Hyde didn't answer, just started down towards the outskirts of the settlement. He knew precisely where to begin. No rearrangement or expansion of the camp could make him forget. If it had been fifty years since he'd last seen the ground, he'd still have been able to recall every inch of it.

The first structures they came to were skeletal affairs hastily erected by the most recent arrivals using only the scantiest supply of flimsy materials. As they threaded their way further in on an erratic course towards the brick-built core of the camp, the shelters became more elaborate. Ingenious use had been made of the most unlikely materials. Oil drums, tarpaulin, wooden pallets, dented jerry cans, anything that could be pressed into use. A clever few had even used fragments of aircraft fuselage looted from crash sites. The luckiest were those who had set up home in the ready-made residences supplied by the gutted shells of knocked-out armoured vehicles that the camp had grown to engulf.

A corner of Hyde's mind saw the ground not as it was now, covered with a litter of human debris, but as it had been during those first wild battles when the Warsaw Pact forces had without warning hurled themselves through the Iron Curtain. Then this had been

82

uncluttered rolling farm land, and the scene of ferocious armoured battles. For ten days the light of burning vehicles had been the only illumination in the smoke and dust that rose so thickly it had turned the days of midsummer into constant night.

Hyde recalled the morning when the battalion of Soviet infantry aboard armoured carriers had been forced into the cover of the woods by repeated air attacks, and totally destroyed by the combined destructive forces of several thousand hastily scattered mines and the firepower of five British anti-tank platoons. And then had come the order, "Board carriers", and they'd charged out into the open to exploit the local victory.

Within a yard or two, Hyde knew he was walking very nearly the same course as his carrier had taken that day. For twenty glorious minutes they had rampaged through the flanks of Russian columns, wiping out one motor-rifle battalion and putting the survivors of two more to flight. Warning had just come through of approaching tanks when they'd collided with an overturned field kitchen trailer and shed a track. Even as the hatches had been thrown open for a bale-out, a sledgehammer blow had crushed in the side armour and a shaft of molten explosives and metal had blasted across the compartment. Hyde remembered the lieutenant's head as it dissolved in the jet of plasma, and the searing terrible heat on his face.

For a moment Revell waited, not knowing why the sergeant had stopped, then he tried to nudge him forward and when that and the following dig in the ribs had failed, leant forward to whisper urgently into his

83

ear. "What have we stopped for? Keep moving."

There wasn't much of it to be seen. A lean-to that had been erected at its rear left only a portion of its rust-streaked side visible between the crowd of sagging hovels that had sprouted up about it. No effort was needed on Hyde's part to recall how it had looked when he'd last seen it, shortly before being picked up and whisked to safety by the crew of a Samaritan armoured ambulance from almost under the tracks of a Soviet T72. The spouts of flame had been boiling from every opening, and burning ammunition had fountained white streamers into the black smoke.

"It's nothing, nothing." He had seen enough, remembered too much. Hyde took his eyes from the sight and his mind from the memory.

There were a few children running about, but not as many as Revell had expected. The camps in Yugoslavia had swarmed with them. Nor was there a single dog to be seen, usually so much a part of the refugee scene.

Attempts had been made by some of the inhabitants to inject if not a note, at least a reminder of civilisation. Plastic flowers, surely one of the few things these people could not put to a more useful secondary purpose, adorned a few of the huts. The one light touch did nothing to hide the utter squalor of the place, or mask its ugliness.

And there was one final aspect of the camp that could not be concealed, the stench from the crude overflowing lavatories spaced out across the area.

An old crone trotted from a side alley and collided heavily with Revell, dropping the large bundle of rags that she carried. Out of sheer habit the major bent down to pick them up for her, and for his trouble was almost slashed across the face by a claw-like wrinkled hand armed with five wicked talons. The nails raked across his clothes, but the hag didn't attempt a second blow; instead she dived down on the bundle, gathered it up and scurried around the trio to depart down another narrow passageway. She tried to spit at Revell as she went, but succeeded only in dribbling down her stained print dress.

"She thought you were going to nick her stuff. We're lucky she didn't start screaming her head off." Anticipating the crone's reaction, Libby had stepped aside. If the Yank wanted to make bloody problems for himself then let him find his own way out of them. You couldn't get through to those tough old women. They were hard as nails and crafty as foxes. Too old to sell themselves, too active to get the special Oxfam rations for the infirm, their lives were a continual race against death. Their every waking moment was spent in search of the means by which they might ensure enough to eat for just another day.

"It's round here, I think." In the middle of a tortuously winding alley Hyde paused and looked about. It would have been a more profitable exercise to map the shifting dunes of a desert than try to remember the layout of one of these metamorphic settlements. A mildewed structure of corrugated asbestos sheets looked familiar. "We'll try down here."

There was room to admit them only in single file, and frequent twists and turns made their previous route as good as an autobahn by comparison.

Hyde raised his hand and they stopped before a

85

rickety hut that was only kept upright by its neighbours. He clenched his fist to rap at the thin wood frame to which the canvas door was fastened, but didn't. Instead he took his knife and, motioning the others to silence, proceeded to cut an opening in the thick fabric.

As he cut the third side of a square a man-sized opening appeared and the material curled down. Stepping into the gloomy interior he signalled the others to follow.

The filthy face and grime-smeared hands, that were all that was visible of the curled form beneath the pile of rags and paper cement bags on the sagging camp bed, blurred into rapid action with an ugly snarl.

Eyes only half accustomed to the gloom made it difficult for Hyde to accurately intercept the pistol produced from beneath the sacking, but the toe of his boot just caught it, and spun it to a far corner.

A howl of rage came from the figure, and then a brief torrent of hate-filled German, before Libby pounced and shoved a wad of cloth into the gaping mouth.

"Shut up, you old cow." With the palm of his hand the sergeant shoved the woman back down on the bed from which she'd half-risen. He pinned her flailing arms to her side and her struggles ceased, but not her muted attempts to tell the intruders what she thought of them and their methods.

"Take it easy, Sergeant. If you reckon she can tell us something, we need her cooperation. Breaking her arms won't get it. Who is she?" There was nothing to give Revell any hint that this was other than just one of

86

the thousands of shelters that made up the camp: or that the old woman was any different from the specimen who'd attempted to claw him shortly before, or any of the hundreds more of her kind who must inhabit the place.

"This is Old Mother Knoke. She's just about the most poisonous old witch in the whole of the Zone." Shred at a time, Hyde pulled out the gag.

As the last piece was removed she opened her toothless mouth, then caught sight of the Makarov 9mm automatic that Libby had retrieved from the corner and was now training on her. Instead of shouting, she began a venom filled monotone of guttural invective.

"In English, you nasty old bitch, in English."

At the words from Hyde she stopped and put her head on one side, like a bird considering the risks before tentatively approaching what could either be a rare tasty morsel or a trap. Her eyes flickered from Hyde to Libby, and then to Revell, on whom they lingered longer, before coming to rest on the sergeant again.

"I know you, Faceless." The lank white hair bobbed up and down as she nodded her recognition. "Have they given up trying to repair you, will they not let you go home like that?" Mother Knoke gave a dry cackle at her own humour, while her sharp grey eyes strayed once more towards the American officer. "Whatever you want it will cost you," again the sly glance at Revell, "a lot."

"You just worry about the payment you'll get if you don't supply what we want."

Again there was the dry rustling laugh as the old

woman digested Libby's threat. "A shot will bring the Russians. There is a post not fifty metres from here." The lop-sided leer with which she concluded the sentence disappeared, as Libby gathered up a handful of mixed cloths and wadded them about the barrel of the pistol.

Feeling a light tap on his shoulder Hyde turned to see Revell's beckoning finger, and went with him to a corner.

"Sergeant, I've gone along with this so far, but will you tell me just what the hell you're up to with this smelly old dame? Just how is she going to help us?"

Hyde checked over his shoulder and saw that Libby and Mother Knoke were still frozen in the same tableau, the swaddled tip of the gun barrel only an inch from the woman's temple.

"You know what it's like in the camps, Major. To survive everyone has to corner some sort of business. Mother Knoke is too wrinkled to sell herself, too lazy to work, so she's developed to a fine art and a decent business what most old women do in a small way and never give a thought to, she's a gossip. There's nothing happens around here she doesn't know about. She knows who comes, who goes, who dies. That's how she lives. If you want to trace a member of your family or find out who's paying the best price for young virgins, or who can get a message out to the West—then you ask Mother Knoke."

"What's it going to cost us?" Much as Revell felt revulsion at being involved in the transaction, there was a practical side in which he had to take an interest. "We're travelling light, apart from our weapons and ammunition, and it appears the old vulture has ways of getting those for herself."

"A lot of them in the camps have got guns. After every battle they're there for the taking. Now and again the Reds have a sweep to try and collar them all, like we do with the camps near us, but these are big places . . . still I suppose we might want to use the grubby hag again, so we'd better sweeten the pill." From a capacious pocket Hyde took out a plastic bag that bulged with a selection of K-rations.

"These are for you, if . . ." Hyde had to snatch the bag out of reach as Mother Knoke, ignoring the pistol trained on her, lunged forward to try and secure the bait, ". . . if you'll tell us all you know about a new Soviet unit operating somewhere around here. The 97th Technical Support Battalion."

Conflict combined with greed and frustration chased across Knoke's dirt-ingrained features. "I not know about army, only refugees." Her hands opened and closed spasmodically as though she longed to snatch the food.

Libby ostentatiously checked the safety catch was off on the pistol, and that a round was chambered, then brought it back to bear on his target.

Again Hyde tantalisingly dangled the powerful persuader. "Don't give me that. You're like a bloody Hoover, you suck up and store every whisper, you know something."

Still the flexing fingers displayed just how much Mother Knoke wanted what was so temptingly offered. There was a note of anguish in her voice as she saw the chance of obtaining the food slipping away. "I do not know, if I did . . ." She had eyes now only for the bag. "I only know about camp."

At random, Hyde extracted a cube of anonymous food from the cache and tossed it to her. He turned to Revell. "She doesn't know anything, not even enough to build a convincing lie around. We might as well do a recce on foot, there's not much chance we'll spot anything, but . . ."

"Hold it a minute. Let me try."

A triumphant look, almost of self-congratulation, leapt into the old woman's face as she caught Revell's accent for the first time. Her suspicions were confirmed, he was an American. She whined. "If I can help . . . I am ill, I need food . . . I can help, I want to help."

Only a warning prod from Libby stopped her lunging forward to grasp Revell's hand, as he sat down on an empty five-gallon disinfectant drum beside the bed.

"Have the Russians been doing any building lately, anything? Within the last two or three months." He didn't need to be a brilliant detective to notice the abject disappointment in Mother Knoke's face as she shook her head.

"No, nothing. Some holes for guns, trenches, like always; and the new drains . . . that is all."

"What drains, where?"

"On the far side, across the camp. They cleared the people out, said they would drain the land, make it healthy, then they would not let them back. They put mines . . . those who tried to return, to take tools, cement, they died."

"Show me where this was." The major thrust a sketch map of the camp and surrounding country under her nose.

She fussed with it. "I am not good with these." Finally a ragged nail stabbed down on a bulge on the east side of the camp.

"Here, have these." Revell took the bag and threw it on to the bed.

Mother Knoke grabbed it before it began to slide off the paper sacks and hugged it to her chest.

"American?" Now cunning joined greed and the other naked emotions that chased across her face. "You have something else, you have lots of everything, yes? Not like tight-arse British." She shook the bag contemptuously at Hyde, but kept a firm hold on it. Deride it she might, lose it she wouldn't.

Getting no hint from Hyde of what was expected, Revell handed over two packs of State Express and what money he had on him, about ninety marks. Mother Knoke didn't count the notes, but stuffed them with the cigarettes into the plastic bag and hugged the mixed payment to her.

"You've told us everything?"

Knoke nodded frantically. "Yes, yes, everything."

"Can I have a go now, Sarge?" Libby pocketed the pistol.

"Make it quick." Hyde had been expecting Libby's request.

Not waiting for the officer's approval, Libby fished out the photograph and thrust it at Knoke. "You know her? Helga Brandt, twenty-five, blonde. She is with an old man, her grandfather, Eric Brandt."

A shrug and averting of her eyes showed Mother Knoke's total lack of interest. She had obtained all she could from these men, there was nothing more to be gained by being helpful in this other matter.

The unconcern turned to sheer terror as the bag was wrenched from her and held beyond her reach. Libby's other hand clenching her around the throat was almost unnoticed, as she struggled to reach the treasures of which she'd so abruptly been deprived.

In the poor half-light of the hovel's interior Revell couldn't see Libby's face, but he knew the soldier was about to squeeze much harder. He leant over, took up the photo from where it had fallen on to the floor and pushed it in front of the woman, blotting out the lost payment from her sight. "Tell him."

"She is pretty. Perhaps she is at the farm."

For a reason the major didn't understand Libby tightened his grip.

"She wouldn't be there, she wouldn't." Libby increased the pressure on the scrawny neck still further. "She's not a tart."

Mother Knoke was fighting for breath. "I do not know her, I would tell . . ."

"That's enough. Pack it in before you choke her." Hyde had to exert a lot of force before he could unlock Libby's fingers and allow the hag to start breathing once more. He restored the plastic bag to her eager hands.

"Won't she squawk the moment we're gone?"

"Not her, Major, not her. If she yaps to the Reds she runs the risk of us being taken alive and telling who gave information about their activities."

"We'll scout this site she's pinpointed, then." Revell

folded the map and put it away. "This is the first real bit of luck we've had."

"And perhaps it isn't."

Where Libby indicated, silhouetted in the improvised opening stood a squatly powerful figure, the stark outline of a Russian submachine gun aimed from its hip.

Chapter Seven

"They've been gone more than three hours. Wonder how much longer they'll be?" Rinehart began to deal yet another hand of poker. He was determined to win back the money and reputation that Cohen had taken off him.

Dooley picked up his cards with only casual interest; he rarely won, but it didn't matter. At every fresh loss he casually scribbled out another marker he had no intention of redeeming. "Yeah, well if that were me with the chance to run loose in one of those camps you'd never see me again, except maybe when I came out every month or so to pick up fresh stores from the PX, so I could keep on buying tail at a can of beans a time."

"You chase tail that's been eating nothing but beans and you'll end up getting your cock blown off." Cohen looked at his hand and adopted a smug expression.

"Yeah, especially the way you like going at them." With a flourish Rinehart laid down a run, then snorted in disgust and disbelief as Cohen revealed four queens. "Fuck this, I've had enough. If these weren't my cards. . . ."

Smiling all around, Cohen scuffed the crumpled notes from the bench and into his helmet. "Such luck, who'd have thought it. Gentlemen, thank you."

"Piss off." The words came out of habit, Dooley wasn't really concerned. He'd lost nothing, nothing real, and he wasn't too bothered about Jango. If the stupid nigger wanted to go chucking his money to the Yid, that was alright with him. He feigned disinterest, but watched carefully as their electronics man sorted the cash out into neat piles and then transferred it to one of the many pockets in his flak jacket. Yeah, it kinda suited him to have all the dough concentrated in the one place. If the little fella bought it, he was going to be the first one to him, and then bonanza, instant riches.

"What's it like in the camps? I've only ever seen them on the news."

"Rather nasty." Clarence sorted through the cleaning rags, looking for one less contaminated by dust and grit than the rest. "They mostly resemble a penguin winter colony. Everyone huddled into a great mass, all trying to work their way to the greater comfort and security of the centre, and finding when they get there that it's all pushing, and shoving and bullying; so they're really no better off at all."

"Hey, that's almost fucking poetic. You sure are cute with words. What'd you do, swallow a dictionary?" Sprawled along a bench, Dooley took up a disproportionate amount of room, forcing Collins into a small corner at its far end.

"No, but I do have the advantage over you of being able to read on the rare occasions when I need to refer to one."

"Reckons he's a real smart arse, don't he?" It took Dooley a moment to realise the nature of the insult.

Cohen didn't share the big man's feeling about the sniper. "I'm not bothered if he's got an IQ of minus ten or plus two hundred. He does his job. Why don't you use some of that hot air you're always spouting to clean the machine gun?"

"Will you listen to this crud. He's been in charge for a few shitty hours and suddenly he reckons he's a three-star general." Sitting up and taking out his cigarette, Dooley offered one to Collins. It was declined, as he'd known it would be. "Ain't you got no vices yet, kid?"

Collins could feel himself going red, and Burke was no help, grinning, enjoying the American's discomforting of him. He made a non-committal noise and fussed with the already fastened buckle of a pack.

"You sure are one hell of an aggravating bastard, Dooley."

"What'd I do now?" Dooley looked aggrieved at Jango's accusation. "I just asked him if he had any bad habits, can't I say anything? You guys cheese me off. I wish I were out there with the Major, screwing my way through the camp. Jesus, I bet he's having one hell of a good time."

The figure took a step inside the doorway, and with a

jerk of the cut-down PPsh-41 submachine gun motioned the three NATO soldiers back against the far wall. Four other figures crowded in, a sixth staying on watch at the door.

Mother Knoke leapt from her bed with astounding agility for her years and threw herself in front of the intruders. Her impassioned torrent of words was swept aside with her as she was roughly pushed back to the bed.

There had been no chance for Revell or Hyde to draw their pistols. Libby's hand had closed on the Makarov he'd taken from the woman, but left it where it was in his pocket. Its eight-round magazine was no match for the firepower ranged against them.

"They're not Commies." By the light streaming in through the door, Hyde could make out the ragged civilian dress of the newcomers.

"Then who the hell are they?" Revell whispered back.

"We are Germans. You would call us deserters, from the Soviet-led forces of the German Democratic Republic, from the puppet army of our Communist oppressors—East Germans."

To Revell it was not so much the fact that he was unexpectedly addressed in English, but that the speaker was female, that surprised him. Very female judging by the outline he saw against the light. He was given no time to ask questions.

Without being searched, all three of them, and Mother Knoke, were herded out into the alleyway, and then along it, closely guarded by their escort. The route provided no opportunity for escape.

They passed the Russian post Mother Knoke had mentioned, a small clearing surrounded by a dense thicket of barbed wire. At its centre stood a low hexagonal concrete structure, beside which stood a tall guyed mast, a throbbing generator and an unattended cooking fire. It was one of the Soviets' jamming stations.

The tight bunched group passed it safely, using a layer of the passing human traffic as cover, the East Germans concealing their truncated submachine guns under drapes of sacking.

Now the camp was wide awake, and there were many more people about. After the departure of those going in search of food or salvage beyond the camp's confines, those who were left behind were mostly inclined to simply sit and stare at the ground, or engage in listless conversation in which it seemed they could summon little interest. There was no other way for them to pass the time that hung so heavily.

There was no other sign of the Russians. Revell wasn't surprised. With most of the Soviets' surplus energy devoted to keeping the various satellite components of the Warsaw Pact armies in line, they had few enough men left to do a bare surveillance job on the camps, let alone police them or organise indoctrination of the inmates beyond the occasional use of loud-speakers. Only the settlement's usefulness as cover for otherwise vulnerable installations prevented the Russians from herding the displaced civilians across the nuclear- and chemical-contaminated territory at the heart of the Zone, to the West.

To fill the void, the running of the camps fell to the

gangs: deserters, criminal elements, the dregs of humanity. They brought not order, but terror, and were capable of matching the Russians themselves when it came to acts of calculated brutality.

An unexpected halt, a flurry of activity that included much pushing and shoving, and Revell found himself inside a derelict barn. Shell holes in the walls had been covered with scraps of cardboard.

The moment they were inside, Mother Knoke restarted her impassioned pleading to their captors, going down on her knees before the stocky shaven-headed individual who appeared to be their leader.

Hyde watched, saw him try to ignore the old woman for a minute, then lose patience and throw her aside. As he did, he saw the plastic bag for the first time.

There was a wail of despair from the woman as it was grabbed from her.

"Brave lump of shit when it's an old girl, aren't you!" Hyde's unmoving visage locked on the ringleader. "Want to try taking something from me?"

A glare and a curled lip was the only immediate reaction from the man. He tossed the bag to the girl who was with them, accompanying it with a growled instruction.

Hyde edged a little closer to Revell. "They haven't got silencers on those things, they're not going to shoot anybody."

"That's not a gamble I'm prepared to take at the moment, let's just play along. If they haven't killed us or at least taken our weapons by now, then they're after something. Let's find out what, before we take them."

Though his German was far from fluent, Libby

100

caught the gist of what the muscled runt had told the girl. He watched her delve into the bag and take out the cigarettes, then hand it back to Mother Knoke. The ringleader had told her to take out any money as well, but she hadn't. Another of the gang snarled a threat at Knoke and then propelled her from the dilapidated building with his boot.

While the rest of the gang kept Revell and his men covered, the leader and girl conferred in a corner. Then she came over and stood in front of the major.

"You are American, they are British." She pointed with her submachine gun. For her small frame the weapon was too large, too ugly. "You have come here to learn something, or do something. We will help you. In return you will take us with you when you go back. It is agreed?"

For all their caution they had been identified and followed, perhaps from the moment they entered the camp. Hyde swore, quietly, under his breath. "Things getting a bit hot for you round here, are they?"

A brief pause while she translated and conferred with bullet-head, and then . . .

"There is nothing else you need to know now. We can help, you know our price."

He couldn't help it: she had a gun on them, was with a band of the nastiest individuals imaginable, and still Revell could look at her and see just a beautiful girl. It was a hard, high-cheeked beauty. Tight jeans that made a dozen arrows of white creases drew his eyes to her crotch; and the dirt-streaked parka she wore, though its quilting revealed only a hint of the breasts beneath, was pulled tight enough to her body to

101

illustrate a tiny waist that emphasised her uncon-
cealable femininity.

"Where is your transport?"

Revell felt relief the instant she translated the hoarse
prompting. While that was still unknown to the East
Germans he held the upper hand.

"If they want to bargain or offer their services, tell
these apes to point those weapons at the floor. I get
rather stubborn when a couple of hundred rounds are
aimed my way." It was a crucial moment. Revell
watched and waited as she translated. Hell, she was
lovely. Jet black hair that framed her face didn't hang
in greasy strips, but fell as separate strands that rested
like a swinging bell on her shoulders. From the rear the
view was just as feminine. Below the hem of her jacket
the tight centre seam of the denim showed off the
halves of her backside.

At last the barrels of the submachine guns were
lowered, though that was as far as the relaxation went.
Fingers remained on triggers, and their guards' attitude
remained one of suspicious vigilance.

"Have you ever worked with this sort of crew
before?" Revell held an urgent whispered conversation
with Hyde.

"Never needed, and never wanted to, Major. I
wouldn't trust any of them, not as far as I could throw
them, and in the case of short-and-fat there," he
indicated the deserters' leader, "that isn't very far."

"We could use them though." Since the loss of
Sergeant Windle and the others of the platoon, Revell
had been only too aware of just how thin on the ground
they were for the task they had been given. And now

102

with the possibility of the workshops being dug in, the chance of extra manpower, and consequently fire-power, had obvious attractions.

"Yes, and we could get shot in the back while the job's in progress, or right after it's finished, if this mob see an advantage in doing that rather than going ahead with the original arrangement." The suspicions in Hyde's mind were, he knew, only too well founded. In the past British patrols had used renegade East German scouts, and the few survivors of those patrols had returned with stories of treachery and ambush.

The major had formed his own evaluation of the offer, and of the individual who made it. He thought little of either, but they needed those extra guns. "How many of you are there altogether?"

"There are just the six of us. We lost five men yesterday when we tried to enter a Russian dump. Some were taken alive, so by now we will be known."

Without question Revell accepted the girl's state-ment. The efficiency of the Russian interrogation methods was well known. Both the military police, the so-called Commandant's Service, and the military arm of the KGB were expert in extracting the truth. Anyone falling into their hands would tell everything before they died. No wonder this handful of renegades wanted out, and their desperation only made them all the less trustworthy.

"You're with them?" Despite the submachine gun, and the familiar way in which she handled it, Revell found it hard to believe that the girl was a full member of this ugly crew.

"Yes. I had been conscripted as a telegraphist into

103

the Territorial Workers Militia. The Soviets killed all our officers, and were sending us to Russia as a labour battalion, because we would not provide a firing squad to shoot civilians who had been stealing from them." She threw a look of contempt at her companions. "I would never work for the Russians, so I ran away. This is as far as I could get."

Hyde had been sidling nearer to the officer while the exchange went on, and now he whispered from behind the hand he held over his lipless mouth. "I've got a smoke grenade. We could be out of here before this lot know what's happening."

Though he didn't hear the words, the shaven-headed East German sensed that something was going on and took a threatening pace forward. He indicated with jerking movements of his submachine gun that he wanted them to move apart.

"Well?" Hyde held his ground.

"No, we can use their firepower. It's our transport they want. I reckon we can trust them until the job's done." Revell spoke to the girl. "Tell your ugly friend we'll do a deal."

While Revell, the girl, and bullet-head held a discussion to iron out the details of the arrangement, Hyde and Libby withdrew to a corner.

"Can't say I'm too keen on this, Sarge. Do you think he knows what he's doing?"

"I bloody hope so. It's not just his neck he's sticking out. Mind you, he's right about them being OK until they find out where the skimmer is; it's after that things could start to get a bit hairy. I wouldn't put anything past this lot."

"I know someone who won't like this arrangement—Clarence." Libby accepted a cigarette and a light from Hyde. "As far as he's concerned, once a Commie always a Commie. He's quite likely to blow their heads off the moment he sees them."

"I can't see the major being too happy about that if it happens. So we'd better keep an eye on him, hadn't *you*?"

The heavy emphasis wasn't lost on Libby. "I'm not his bloody keeper."

"You are now. I'm not having this job and my pension buggered up, just because one of my blokes takes it into his head to shoot GDR deserters into decent imitations of lace curtains with dum-dums. Anyway, you're the only one he really gets on with."

That was something Libby could not deny. He and Clarence had lost much in the war. For the sniper though the loss of his family, a part of his mind and his humanity at least had been sudden and complete. For Libby fate had reserved a more spiteful piece of cruelty. Two days before he and Helga were to be married, the Russian armour had plunged into West Germany: the border town of Ratzburg where she lived with her grandfather had been one of the first to be overrun. All he could do now was keep looking and hoping. To do so he had to stay in the Zone, and he'd stay there for as long as it continued to exist, and he lived.

Revell concluded his discussion through their interpreter and rejoined Hyde.

"He's called Kurt." Revell indicated the leading deserter. "He says he is, or rather was, a captain in the 8th GDR Motor Rifle Division."

"The hell he was."

"I agree with you, Sergeant. Those weapons they're carrying must be the ones they had when they went over the hill, and the only units I know of that were still issued with those antiquated pieces when the war started were the Grepos, the border police."

"We're not in very nice company, then, are we. I wonder how the girl got mixed up with them." The more Libby saw of her, the more she reminded him of Helga. It was the stance she adopted, her air of determination, independence, Helga's qualities, the reasons he felt sure she must still be alive.

"Who knows. Maybe you'll get the chance to ask her. They're going to show us exactly where the Russians were doing their digging. You don't seem at all happy with the idea, Sergeant Hyde."

The Yank was a perceptive bastard, Hyde had to give him that. How do you tell an officer you reckon he needs his bleeding brains tested? "It's your decision, Major, but there's a couple of precautions I think we should take while they're around."

"OK, I'm listening."

"Main thing is to keep an eye on Kurt. If any trouble starts he'll be the one to fire first. And don't let them bunch us together. Stay spread out among them, that way we'll make less of a target if they try any funny business."

"That's a nice comforting thought." Libby deliberately lengthened a tear in his ragged overclothes to make access to his pistol and grenades easier. It was a bloody stupid way of going to war: dressed like a tramp, working with scum who probably didn't even trust each other and certainly couldn't be trusted by

106

anyone else. That was the Zone, slowly destroying even those it didn't kill, grinding them lower and lower to a sub-human level where any action was acceptable or justifiable. But these men were border police, men who'd earned bonus payments for each would-be escaper through the Iron Curtain that they shot down. They had a head start on everyone else.

Chapter Eight

"Can't you do something to keep him quiet. Give him another jab, two if it'll help." The intermittent screams from the wounded man were beginning to fray Burke's nerves.

"What do you want me to do, gag him?" Rinehart was becoming irritated by the constant interference. "He's had an extra shot already, but it doesn't do any good, not with the skull fractures he's got."

"That's not bloody fractures, half his bloody head is shot away. Why don't you save him a lot of pain, get it over with now?"

The black had to wait until Nelson had finished another sequence of wailing and incoherent shouting before his reply could be heard. "In our outfit we don't pull the plug on nobody, not even a specimen like you."

"I would, if it were him." Dooley grinned broadly at Burke.

Cohen stepped back inside. He'd gone out on to the ramp for a while to get away from the bickering, and smell of sweat and blood and stale tobacco. There was little movement of air about the skimmer. Even with every hatch and port open, the fetid atmosphere inside was hardly stirred by the light breeze that ruffled the tops of the oaks.

"I've counted. Between you, you've managed to start fifteen arguments in the five hours since the major left. Maybe you want to try for sixteen?" No one took Cohen up. "You want to get some air, kid, you're starting to look a bit green about the gills." He moved aside to let Collins squeeze past. "Don't step off the ramp. If you want to have a pee you'll have to do it from there, anything else you'll have to hang on to. I've spotted a suspicious lump below that might react rather loudly to having a pile of shit dropped on it."

"You sure are taking this being left in charge thing seriously. I ain't never even heard an officer telling anyone how to crap. Hey, can you imagine that?" The idea appealed to Dooley, and he offered it to the general audience. "On the command, wait for it, pants down. Shitting commences now. Arse paper will only be torn off from left to right . . ."

An outburst of yelling from Nelson blotted out his finale. As the wounded man's shouts tailed away, and the wracking arching spasm that had accompanied it subsided, before Dooley could repeat his last words, there was the sound of cannon fire.

"Light stuff." Like the others Burke froze in his seat as he listened intently, trying to identify the type and direction of fire. "North of the woods, so it's not between us and the major."

"That's Commie flak, twin 23mm mount by the sound of it." There was another noise Rinehart could detect between the rapid bursts. Faint at first, but growing louder, a high-pitched buzzing like a disturbed bee-hive. No, more like the engine of a model aircraft. "Hell, it's an RPV, a sky-spy."

Even as he said it, at the end of a sustained rattle of cannon fire the tinny note changed, became ragged.

Still on the ramp, Collins looked up and saw the miniature craft for an instant as it flashed overhead. Looking like a six-foot-diameter discus with a lift fan set in its centre, the dappled white-and-blue remotely piloted reconnaissance vehicle swished a leaf-chopping path across the treetops as it plunged towards the ground. The cloudless sky could be seen through a large dark-edged hole near its rim, from which spun a trail of vaporising fuel. "That's one of ours."

"What the hell do they think they're playing at?" Rinehart fumed. "We want the Ruskies around here lulled to sleep, not kept awake and damned well encouraged to shoot at anything that moves. Shit, what did they expect to see, us in full blazing action?"

"That I don't know." A heavy impact among the trees a few hundred yards away punctuated Cohen's words. "If it was just fitted out for recording and retrieval then they won't get anything anyway; sounds like it just piled in. But, if it was one of the new ones with a real-time transmitter, then there's a fair chance that Ol' Foul Mouth and an assortment of brass have just had a close-up of the kids' weapon in action."

For a moment Collins was about to ask what he meant, then he recalled why he'd been out on the ramp. He sought a way in which to hide his embarrassment. "Will they come to look for it?"

"Who, the Reds? No way. I got a brother in the electrical business in Chicago, if he knew he might

111

make the journey, he deals in a lot of second-hand, but the Russians, no. They must bring down five or ten every day in this sector alone. Unless one falls on a Commissar I shouldn't think they give it a second thought, maybe not even then. It's like my sun-tanned friend says, it'd just be better if all the Commie gun crews got their heads down while we went about their business."

"I reckon we'll get a medal if we pull this off." Dooley lit up at the thought. "Maybe they'll ship us back home to the States and put us on TV. I could get my picture in the paper."

"Have to be a double page spread to get your head in."

Ignoring Cohen, the big man went on building his dream. "Hey, I'd be famous, like, like . . ." he sought examples, "like, like . . ."

"Godzilla, King Kong, Hitler, Attila The Hun?"

He was not about to be put down. "Just think of it, all those beautiful broads who'd love to be shafted by a big hero like me."

"Some hope, brother, some hope." There was deep scorn in Rinehart's laugh. "Do we live in the same world, we fighting the same war? The only way that'd happen is if we carved our way to Moscow and stomped the Kremlin flat with our bare feet. Trips home are for officers and cripples: medals are for guys who look good in the papers. And as for that screwing, what have you got to offer? OK, you don't have to show me . . . so you got a tool that wouldn't disgrace a stud stallion, but a decent piece wants more than that. Like always, it's the guys who stayed home and made the tanks and missiles that have got all the money and

112

they'll get all the action. When we go back, if ever, we'll be treated like we carried plague. People have heard so much about radiation counts, bacterial weapons, no one will come within a mile of us, and even your cock won't reach that far."

"Shame, isn't it." Burke had enjoyed watching Dooley's bubbles being shot down. "Still, that's America for you."

"Since when have you Brits had so much to crow about?" The jibe stung Cohen into a swift rejoiner. "If we weren't supplying more than half your equipment, you'd be down to using sling shots by now. You got so many fellow travellers on your little island it's a wonder you didn't open the doors to the Commies a year ago. Is going on strike still your main sport, or have you invented some new way of losing the war?"

"We've locked up all the rubbish now, and striking has been illegal for nine months," Burke waded back in.

"Pulling little girls' panties down has always been, but that still goes on." There was more aggravation to be milked from the exchange, and Dooley went after it. "You're just lucky we're always around to bail you out."

"Would you care to step outside and say that, loud-mouth." It was Clarence's voice, floating down from the turret where he'd been listening.

He was half out of his seat, ready to accept the challenge before Dooley saw the expressions about him, and settled back down. "Very funny. Save it for another time."

Clarence dropped from the turret. "What a pity. I thought you'd go bouncing out into the minefield. Ah

113

well, never mind, it almost worked." He hauled himself back to his aerie and resumed his slow cranking of the manual turret traverse.

"Don't that creep ever get dizzy?" With a jerk of his thumb Dooley indicated the steadily rotating lower trunk and legs. "It ain't like he can see anything, except the damned trees and a few wrecks. Is he bucking for a stripe or what?"

"You wouldn't catch me doing any work I didn't have to." Burke found a sentiment he could wholeheartedly agree with in Dooley's words.

"That I had already worked out for myself." Cohen nodded.

"Well what's the point in knocking yourself out. I've got enough to do with driving the Cow, and looking after it. I don't need any more work."

"So how about doing the work you've got." Seeing his remark ignored Cohen added a rider that would carry more weight, and the rest of the crew with him. "When we have to move out, it's going to be in a hurry. There won't be any time to get out and tighten up a few nuts and bolts; so how about you check this old clunker over, especially that damaged motor. Stay on the hull, keep your feet off the ground and you'll be safe enough."

Put that way Burke couldn't refuse, not with the eyes of all the others on him. With ill grace he grabbed up a tool roll and went out.

Rinehart watched their driver haul himself up out of sight on to the roof. "It sure has gone quiet in here, but I ain't gonna miss him for the next hour or so. I think I'll just catch some shut-eye."

"After you've changed Nelson's dressing." Cohen

114

saw the smirk on Dooley's features as the black had to give up the corner in which he'd just made himself comfortable. "You want a job?"

"You going to give me one? I told you to knock off the officer bit, I ain't impressed."

"No. No, for you I've got no job. What's the point. Big thick stiff like you, what's it matter if when we go into action that old M60 of yours jams up. So you buy it, so what, good riddance."

A growl was Dooley's only response, as Cohen ignored him and fiddled with a strap on his body armour.

Begrudgingly, the big man at last reached for the machine gun and began to strip it.

"Is there something for me to do?"

"You religious, you believe in the power of prayer?"

Collins didn't know what to make of the question. He answered hesitatingly. "Eh, I hadn't really thought . . . I suppose . . . well I haven't . . . not for a long . . . no, not really."

"Pity, that rules out the one useful thing you could have done. OK, so I'm kidding. Help the Hulk with his toy. He'll show you thirty different wrong ways to reassemble an M60."

The hasty softening amendment he tacked on to the slap-down had come almost unconsciously from Cohen. Thirteen months he'd been in the Zone, he was a veteran already. His first day of combat seemed a lifetime away. But it wasn't so far back that he couldn't remember what it was like to be the rookie in a squad. This British boy was no different; the butt of all the humour, the recipient of all the dirty chores. Not that he was making it any easier for the kid. The hardening process, the acquiring of the tough shell that would at last get him accepted as a member of the team, would only take longer if he didn't take all the knocks as they fell due.

"Don't you listen to him, kid. There ain't nothing I don't know about this piece." Dooley's hand flew the practised ritual of disassembly. "Only thing you've got to watch with these is that you don't put the piston back in the cylinder the wrong way round. If you do, the gas ports don't line up and she'll only fire once before stopping. That's not even in the Tech. Manual, but we ain't going that far, not as we might want to slap this old Betsy back together in a hurry if any Ivans come prowling." He held the barrel up to the light and squinted up it. "I wish I were with the major and that three-stripe horror show right now. I'd be looking up a fuck-sight more interesting hole than this."

Rinehart paused from applying a fresh set of dressings to Nelson's shattered cranium. "I reckon that's just wishful thinking. Whatever the major is doing now, he ain't within a hundred yards of a nice slice of tail."

Her name was Andrea; that and what she had told him earlier about her reasons for being there was all he knew about her. There had been no further opportunity to ask questions. The camp was now wide awake and every path was sprinkled with its quota of scruffy hollow-cheeked people. Some slithered slowly through the dust on seemingly aimless journeys, others sat or squabbled or loitered. Each had the half furtive, half apathetic expression that only life, or rather

116

existence, in the camps could induce.

They passed through the little graveyard behind the church. In every corner there were heaps of mouldering bones. The press for living space was so great, the need to find shelter so urgent, that the vaults and tombs had been opened and their long dead occupants replaced by a mass of the half living.

A few paces more and they stepped into the main and only street of the village about which the camp sprawled.

The ground floors of the houses were hidden behind the numberless lean-tos that slumped against their walls. Some brave or desperate souls had even risked adding a second storey to those extensions. The glass had gone from every window, and all of the lower, and some of the upper windows were being used as secondary entrances.

"Over one hundred in that one." Andrea indicated a small cottage that couldn't possibly have boasted more than six rooms, including the kitchen extension. "There are others, detached, not much bigger, that hold twice that number. Many can live in a garage, a whole family in a tool shed."

There was bitterness in her voice. Her whispered words conveyed it clearly and it wasn't lost on Revell. Kurt and the other Grepos took no interest in what went on around them, save anything that had a bearing on their safety. The girl saw everything, and felt it. It was as though she was storing images, locking each into her memory for a future time.

Revell found himself deliberately falling a couple of paces behind her, to get another look at her denim-wrapped backside. She was lovely. What could be her

117

relationship with the loutish Kurt and the others? Not for a moment could he believe that she stayed with them for any reason other than pure convenience. They stank, and their crudely chopped hair and beards added to their uncouth appearance.

A sudden halt was called. Ahead of them an Oxfam Leyland truck was parked in the centre of the street, and from its open back a pair of harassed young men were trying to distribute packets of food to the seething fast-growing crowd surrounding it. Two Russian soldiers wearing the insignia of the Commandant's Service stood nearby, but made no move to instil order. The mass of people about the Leyland surged back and forth.

An elderly man wriggled clear of the press, hugging a tattered prize, only to be knocked down and robbed of it by two heavily built women who began to fight between themselves for possession, even as they waddled away between the buildings. The Russians smirked, and one grunted an ugly laugh. Neither made any move to assist the oldster who had fallen almost at their feet, and was now struggling to get up, blood pouring from his nose and mouth.

Only a gruff warning from Kurt prevented Andrea from using the submachine gun she carried inside the roll of sacking. A colour had risen in her cheeks and when Kurt put out his hand as a further restraint, she shrugged it violently aside.

It was clear to Revell that her distaste for Kurt was almost as intense as her hatred of the Russians. As they took a side turning to avoid the blockage and were once more forced into single file by the narrowness of the route, he found himself behind her again.

She really was something special. He enjoyed looking at women, could find something to appreciate in almost any who weren't too old or dirty, or too gawkily young. The smoothness of the plump ones, the bodies of the plain, the faces of the thin. Every woman had something, but this one, Andrea, harshly beautiful and beautifully built, what a combination! It was a hell of a time to come across a woman with those sort of qualities. Another time, another place, he'd have made a play for her right away. Maybe there'd be a chance to get to know her later on, maybe. So many "maybes", and that was one too many.

Hyde was taking careful note of every inch of their journey. Despite the continuous twists and turns they were holding a generally easterly course: he'd been expecting that. None of the refugees would ever go foraging in that direction, that way led further into Communist held territory. If the Reds were using a part of the camp as cover for their tank repair shops then the eastern sector would be an obvious choice, easier to keep private.

It was also obvious why the East Germans knew about what was, on the surface, an abortive piece of civil engineering. Like Mother Knoke they had a vested interest in knowing everything that went on, in particular where Russians were to be found at any given time. You can't hide until you know where the seeker might be.

The middday sun drew the last wisps of stench from every latrine and pile of refuse. Dust hung in the still air for minutes after it had been raised, and added to the discomforts Libby was already experiencing under his several layers of clothing. Sweat poured from him and combined with the penetrating particles of grit to irritate him to the point of madness. God, he loathed these places. Bitter cold, stifling heat; they never seemed to enjoy a happy medium, and the huts gave little comfort or protection. He looked up at the sound of a jet aircraft approaching, but though it was low enough for the thunder of its passing to bring falls of accumulated dust from the tattered eaves of the huts it was invisible against the sun, and he had to seek and look at shadow for a while before he could blink his eyes clear of the tears brought on by the glare.

It was a relief when Kurt stopped before a shack fashioned from innumerable cardboard boxes bearing assorted brand names, all of them faded and many on the verge of disintegration, and ushered them in.

There was a man and a woman inside, and they scuttled into a corner to hide the object they'd been bent over. But they weren't fast enough to prevent Revell from identifying the partially skinned carcase of a mongrel dog. A pan full of fly blown entrails, a pile of imperfectly cured skins in a corner and dark sinewy strips of meat hanging to smoke over a slow fire gave further proof of the frightened couple's line of business.

Kurt ignored them and their trade, save to snatch a still red-raw strip from the rack, and with his knife opened a thin and fragile wall to make a way into the adjoining hut. He led them in a similar manner through two more, both empty of inhabitants, before making a smaller slit in the patched canvas outer wall of the fourth. That done, he tore off a chunk of the dog meat with his blackened teeth and stood aside with a gesture that invited Revell to look out.

A clearing fifty yards wide stretched away to left and

right, separating a cluster of several hundred shelters, that lay in a hollow between a crescent of low hills, from the main body of the camp.

"What the hell have they done that for?" Libby had found a vantage point of his own and like the officer and NCO was making a survey.

"Could be a fire break." Using his bayonet Hyde made another hole in the canvas at a more convenient height than the one he'd found ready-made.

"Possibly, but look." To either side Revell could see no evidence of the debris of the flattened shelters having been removed or disturbed.

"Looks like they just bulldozed everything flat." A glint of metal caught Hyde's attention. He borrowed the binoculars for a closer examination. "And I mean everything. There's cooking pans, clothes . . . that's all these poor sods have got in most cases. They must have been chucked out fast. I wonder why they didn't go back for them afterwards. This lot of scavengers would have cleared the ground down to bare soil in a matter of hours."

"Follow that wire." Very carefully Revell nudged the binoculars to bring into the sergeant's field of vision a tangled flattened web of slotted angle iron, to which portions of the corrugated plastic sheets that had once formed walls were still attached.

Hyde adjusted the focus, picked up the dull metal thread and panned along it until it vanished in a low heap of mixed debris. The overhead sun illuminated sufficient of the mound's interior for him to recognise the flask-shaped devise nestling there.

"A bloody minefield." Flicking the glasses back and forth, Hyde identified a dozen more of the trip-wires.

"They look directional to me." Revell accepted the binoculars back. "Set to throw their fragments along the clearing, but I shouldn't imagine the Reds are too fussy about what might spray out into the camp. This sheet," he tapped the canvas, "has a few holes that look about the right size." Again he flicked the thick material, where quarter and eight inch diameter holes admitted beams of light that streamed like miniature searchlights across the hovel's dark interior.

"Many did go back." Andrea crossed to stand by Revell, as though she might look out, but she didn't. "The Russians did not stop or warn them. They let the mines do it. Everyone who has tried has been killed, even those who had been in the army and thought they could deal with the mines. They go off if you touch the wires, and there are others that go off for no reason when you are near."

"They wouldn't take that sort of trouble for a few bags of cement, Major. There must be more in there than some unfinished drains."

Revell nodded agreement. "I think you're right, Sergeant Hyde. We still need more information, but I think we just found our target."

Chapter Nine

It was so damned frustrating. Revell panned the binoculars across the clearing and then over the eye-confusing clutter of the detached portion of the camp. There was nothing more to be learnt from their present position.

The few outward signs of the minefield gave every indication of its having been most carefully laid. On their own, the criss-crossing trip-wires would have provided a major and time-consuming hazard to safe clearance, but there were other, more subtle indicators that various different types of mine were also in use. In places there appeared to be inviting gaps in the network of wires; Revell didn't doubt they were a deliberate invitation to the unwary. Pressure, noise, vibration, any one of a dozen stimuli might set off the traps beneath the seemingly safe lanes. They had neither the time, nor the expertise to clear a way through.

Hyde had been considering the same problem. "No way past that lot, Major, not in one piece, and I should imagine it goes all around the place."

123

Only half listening to the sergeant, Revell swept the glasses upward to the bare gentle slopes of the surrounding hills. "We need to find somewhere up there, where we can keep watch for a while and try and figure out the layout of the place."

"It'll have to give good cover." There was no enthusiasm in Libby's voice for the idea. "If this is the place we think it is, then the Ruskies aren't going to take too kindly to having bunches of sightseers gawping at it."

"Now where the hell did they come from?" Coming down through the long grass away to their left Revell saw a group of Russian soldiers. They were lounging along, some indulging in horseplay, all of them carrying their jackets in a casual manner, though as they neared the bottom of the slope, just before they disappeared from sight behind the detached part of the camp, they had begun to dress and tidy themselves.

"Look at the top of the hill . . . no, more to your right, that's it." Under the sergeant's guidance, Revell brought the grey tiled rooftop into his field of vision. That was all that was visible of the building that lay just over the crest.

"It's the Reds' knocking shop, you'd call it a cat-house. Round here it's known as The Farm."

At Hyde's words Andrea stopped fanning herself with the opened front of her jacket and looked at her watch. "The Russian pigs allow the girls to sleep in the afternoon. That will be the last of them leaving now. They have stayed late today. The whores will not be at their best tonight."

"Be an ideal place from which to keep an eye on those workshops, if that's what they are."

"You still have doubts then, Major?" Libby borrowed the glasses.

"We have to be sure. The Reds will only give us the one crack at a stunt like this. If we screw up and all we hit is a field kitchen or mobile bath unit, we'll not only get blasted for a big fat zero, we'll screw it up for the poor SOBs who have to come along after us and try for the real thing. Even if it is the outfit we're looking for, I don't want us to go charging in and shoot up a handful of empty bays and a couple of junked soft-skins. Surprise is the only compensation we have for lack of numbers. At the speed we'll have to get in and out there won't be time to hunt for targets, we have to hit them where it hurts first time." He looked at Andrea. She had closed her jacket again, that was a pity. He had enjoyed watching the twin swells of her high breasts.

"Are you sure about the Ruskies clearing out of that place in the afternoon?"

"That is how it has always been. I do not think they change it."

"You know the place, Sergeant. Are there any problems in walking in there and staying low until we're ready to make our move?"

"Not that I can think of, Major. There's just the one building. Front and back door. Central staircase. Six rooms upstairs, five down. There's a big attic which runs the length of the roof and a small cellar."

"Are there any Russian units close by?"

This time the girl had to refer the query to Kurt; he didn't bother to reply, just shook his head.

"Do you know of any commander, in any army, Major, who'd build a barracks close to a brothel?"

"Can't say I do, Sergeant Hyde, but I can think of a

few Staff Officers who'd make sure the HQ was next door to one." If Hyde had tried to score a point there, Revell hadn't let him. It was difficult to tell when the NCO was being sarcastic and when he wasn't.

Hyde had meant his remark to be a light one, but it had not come out that way. For all this Yank's drive and efficiency, and determination to be in the forefront of the action, Hyde was beginning to take a dislike to him. He was too bloody asustere, even the outwardly flippant counter he'd made to Hyde's question had been delivered without a trace of humorous intent. It was difficult, no impossible, to imagine what the American officer did when he wasn't on duty. Did he sit and play solo all day, stand to attention in a cupboard until it was time to go back on duty again?

Oh sod it. Why couldn't they have left him and Clarence and the others happily potting away at Russian tanks and crews in the salient? Was it simply fate, or the malice of some nameless clerk he'd crossed at battalion HQ that had got him involved in this half-wit scheme?

Well he was lumbered with it now, but if he came through it alright then there was no chance of his doing it again. Soon as it was over he'd rejoin his own outfit like a shot.

More than anything he wanted to stay in the army. What was there for him outside looking like he did, sweet fuck-all. Staying in would probably kill him; getting out, back into civilian life would slowly destroy him. Of the two he much preferred the quicker death and fuller life before it, than the living death and no life at all that would be his lot back home: but by Christ he'd risk it rather than work with these Yanks again, or

126

a moment longer than he had to. First of all though he had to survive. He'd already proved he was good at that; he ran his hands over his facial scars, well fair. In the next twelve hours, the way things were shaping up he'd have to be ruddy brilliant.

The farmhouse stood in isolation in a small fold just below the crest of a softly sloping hill. A single, substantial, stone building devoid of any frills, the area to its front was roughly paved, and beside and behind it stood, sagged or lay the weather-beaten remains of a collection of various sheds and outhouses. The whole was surrounded by a low stone wall.

Kurt had sent his men to watch the back of the house, while he and Andrea with Libby, Hyde and Revell openly approached the front.

Libby noticed the heaps of broken bottles below each window; the piles were substantial. The Russian visitors appeared to have found a fast and presumably amusing way of disposing of their empties. There was glass in every window of the house, and all the curtains were drawn. Even in bright sunshine it was a grim-looking place. The unwanted recollection of Old Mother Knoke's words, "perhaps she's at The Farm" made anger rise inside him. This was one of the ugliest things about the Zone. Many of the women in there were carrying on the trade they'd practised before they'd come to the camp, before the war even: but a number would have been forced into it. He watched while Kurt sorted an intact bottle from the nearest heap and then hammered on the door.

It was a good act, drawn most probably from

127

considerable personal experience. Hyde watched as Kurt bawled and sang and slurred pathetic pleas to the unseen inmates. When he backed off a pace to see if the German's performance had drawn anyone to an upstairs window, Hyde saw for the first time the rear end of a drab painted Mercedes saloon, just discernible in the gloom of a rotting tractor shed. As he drew Revell's attention to it, the boot and knuckle-scarred door swung open.

Before the dressing gown clad woman had time to launch fully into her tirade, Kurt had hurled himself past her and was dashing for the stairs.

Andrea followed, unwrapping her submachine gun as she ran. As Revell and Hyde took one side of the ground floor Libby went to the other. The first two rooms he hurled himself into were empty. He crashed open the third to discover a pair of Russian officers hastily pulling on their pants. One of them already held a pistol, Libby gave him no chance to use it, his second and third shot tearing out the Russian's throat. Blood splashed across the room as the 9mm bullets struck and the dying officer toppled back over a chair to crumple into an untidy heap.

Neither Libby nor the surviving officer paid any attention to the ugly bubblings and rattlings coming from the expiring man. There was another sound in the room, an animal-like whimpering from the heavy breasted girl with thickly caked-on make-up who crouched under the dining table, trying at once both to make herself inconspicuous and frantically gather up and conceal her pendulous breasts.

Insignia on the two crumpled jackets tossed carelessly over the arm of a small sofa indicated that both the visitors were captains. The remaining Russian slowly lowered to the ground the raised leg with which he had frozen, stork like, in the act of dressing on Libby's precipitate entrance, and straightened up. He was well into middle age and the heavy flesh on his stocky body fell in multiple folds about his waist. A mass of dark hair covered his torso and upper legs, and overlong arms gave him an ape-like look that was accentuated by broad slab cheeks, a small nose and deep set eyes beneath thick eyebrows.

The killing had drained Libby's anger, most of it, then the girl whimpered again and he saw her mass of livid bruises and the white mess about her mouth. He retched, and levelled the Browning again.

The Russian saw the look on his attacker's face and clamped his hands in front of his genitals as though he could somehow protect them from what was coming. He saw the knuckle on the trigger whiten and his bowels emptied violently and noisily.

"No ... damn it ... no." Revell's shout blended with the roar of the weapon's firing.

All four bullets struck their target, the last two chasing a dead body as it was spun round and thrown back, fountaining urine and dark red vomit. A limp arm smacked into and cracked one of the panes as the punctured cadaver thumped down below a window, head lolling, sightless eyes contemplating a protruding rib.

"What the hell do you think this is, a butcher's shop?" Revell crossed the room avoiding the stinking puddles and picked up one of the jackets. "You see this, you see this." He waved it under Libby's nose. "These are, were technical support troops, probably from the

97th. They could have told us everything we wanted. What bloody good are they now?"

The sights and smells in the room did not bother Andrea. She stood in the doorway and looked at the bodies. "The only good Russian is a dead Russian. I would say that they are now very good." With no great gentleness she hauled the terrified girl from her hiding place and dragged her from the room. "I will put her with the others."

Libby offered no explanation, no apology.

"Oh, what the hell. It's too late now. Get yourself to an upstairs window and watch out for any Commies that look like they're coming to investigate your executions. Don't open fire until I say, just let me know if you see any. Have I spelt it out clear enough for you?"

"Killing them has become a habit, Major." Hyde appeared and stepped in fast to pre-empt any response from Libby. "It takes a lot of breaking. We haven't taken prisoners for five months, not since we saw Commie tanks gunning down some of our blokes who ran out of ammo and tried to surrender." As the officer did not appear to have been placated, he changed the subject. "All the girls have been herded into one of the big front bedrooms. They're a bit indignant about the whole business, but they're keeping quiet so far."

"OK, let's see if we can find anything out from them. There's nothing to be learnt from these two, and this stink is incredible."

They closed the door after them, passed one of the East Germans who was standing guard by the partially open front door and mounted to the upper floor.

"Girls" was a rather generous description for the

130

collection of variously aged whores who sat on the double-bed and bare boards under Kurt's submachine gun and Andrea's contemptuous glare. Their ages ranged from what might have been about twenty, but looked older, in the case of the girl they'd discovered downstairs, to what in one case might have been getting on for sixty. Most of them appeared to have been in bed, or undressing when the break-in occurred. Only two of the fifteen were wearing more than underclothes beneath the blankets and robes they had pulled about themselves.

The girl who had witnessed Libby's work was sobbing deeply, on the verge of hysterics. Her face had been cleaned up, and with the mess had gone most of her over-done make-up. Her unadorned face was pale and puffy, but not unattractive. Huge breasts and the partial crescent of one large pink nipple bulged over the top of the inadequate sheet with which she'd been provided.

"I want to ask them some questions, Andrea. Tell them we won't hurt them, and we'll see the Russians don't." That was an easy promise to make: Revell had no idea if he could keep it.

The message, though not delivered by Andrea with any grace, or in a friendly tone, had the effect of calming the women. One or two even managed a coy smile at Revell.

Hyde hadn't expected any of them to try their allure on him, and he was right, they didn't. One thing did please him though, he noticed a subtle change come over the major when he started to deal with the women. It wasn't much, a slight softening of his manner and an almost imperceptible shading of his aggressively

American accent. Well, well, well; so the stiff bastard did have a weakness, fancied himself as a ladies man, did he? He had to admit though, it did appear to be working. Although Revell had in most cases to work through a third party, he still contrived to give the impression that he was talking intimately and secretively with each of the whores. Not that Hyde felt himself in any position to criticise or comment on another man's technique, not with the sort of silly-arse games he had to play before any but the roughest drunken scrubbers would have anything to do with him.

"Any good, Major?" The interest was genuine, but it wasn't simply that which prompted Hyde.

"You know it wasn't. They say they don't know a damned thing, that they've never heard of the 97th."

"They probably haven't. The Ruskies who come up here are after a good screw or whatever else it is they fancy, not polite conversation. Did you ask them if they'd heard any movement at night?"

"Of course I damned well did." A note of irritability had crept into the officer's voice. "They've heard trucks and tanks, but that doesn't mean a thing; the Reds do all their resupplying and troop movements at night, same as we do. Could be anything."

"So where do we go from here?"

Revell jerked his thumb at the ceiling. "Up, into the roof. We'll knock out a couple of roof tiles and see what we can from there. As soon as we've got a rough idea of the layout, we'll sketch out a plan and you can go back for the others."

"What about this crowd?"

For a moment Revell gave it consideration. A leer he noticed on the face of one of the East Germans helped him to make a decision. "Get Libby in here. We'll put the deserters on look-out. We don't owe them anything much, no reasons why we should lay on an orgy for them."

"What about her?"

Andrea looked up sharply, "I go where I like, when I like."

It was a temptation, ridiculous but strong nevertheless, to Revell to put her over his knee and give that tight wrapped backside a couple of good hard slaps. Just the thought made his palm tingle as though he had, adding an extra thrust to the erection the scantily clad whores had already begun to excite. In any other than this dangerous situation he'd have found an excuse to get her alone for a while but there wasn't time for that now. Shit, why was it that every attractive, and a lot of the not so attractive girls made him feel like that. His wife had told him his needs, his demands, were one of the main reasons for the break-up of their marriage, though she'd not had the courage to cite them as grounds. Well now she'd got what she wanted, a nice steady twice-a-month-and-have-you-had-a-bath-since-your-last-eh-eh-time-of-the-eh-month-dear. Was he over-sexed? Damn it, it was no time to be pondering that again.

One of the women on the floor had been trying hard to catch Revell's eye. So far he'd avoided it, but when Hyde went out, followed shortly afterwards by Andrea, he had no one to talk to and nowhere else to look.

She was in her late thirties he guessed, with a face that was beginning to show heavy pouches under her eyes, which combined with too much liner made them startlingly dark and intense. A loosely tied gown revealed an ample cleavage, the big orbs jostling against each other at her every movement. The gaping garment didn't meet until it had also revealed the upper of what looked like several rolls of flab about her middle. Her knees were partially drawn up in front of her, and the instant she saw she had the major's attention she slowly parted them to expose a luxuriant mass of pubic hair that hid any detail.

When she realised Kurt was also getting a good look, the limbs were hurriedly clamped together, and the quilted gown once more draped across.

The elbow that poked into his side was Kurt's. The smell of unwashed flesh and dirty underwear made Revell take a pace to one side, not that the Grepo noticed the involuntary reaction, he was far too busy ogling the women.

"Sehr gut, eh? Sehr gut."

Laughter from the other men greeted Kurt's crude pantomime translation as he put a hairy-backed hand to his crotch and simulated a masturbating motion.

In a way though Revell agreed. In different circumstances the whore might have been attractive, but her lifestyle had aged her. To Kurt's tastes doubtless she still was "very good", not for him though. Not with the risk of disease she carried, and the record of the thousands of gross obscenities she had performed with regiments of men etched into her face.

Another of the whores, the oldest one, with the beginnings of a moustache, was turning on her dubious

134

charms for his benefit. To avoid having to look at the flaccid flesh being rearranged and heaved into view for his delectation he went to the door and called out to Hyde. As he did he heard Kurt's throaty chuckle leading the other men into laughter. He suspected it was aimed at his back.

"Sergeant Hyde. I want Libby in here now. Get a move on."

Sat on the floor a little way along the corridor Andrea was checking the contents of four spare magazines for her submachine gun. She looked up at his shout.

As her beautiful eyes flickered over his face Revell felt certain she could read his thoughts, understood his real reason for coming out of the room. What she said tended to confirm that impression.

"There are ugly people in the Zone. Not all of them are Russian."

Chapter Ten

"I love these." Dooley unsheathed the bayonet and held it up, so that the shafts of sunlight filtering in glinted on the mirror polished blade. "They make a fucking lovely sound as you pull them out, sort of a sucking noise. You can't always hear it because of the fuss the crud you stuck it in is making, but sometimes the shits go dead quiet," he nudged Jango with his elbow. "You get it, dead quiet; dead . . . dead quiet. Hey, that's a joke. You like it? I just made it up."

"We'd never have guessed."

"Go back to mending the tele, Cohen, I weren't talking to you. What was I saying?" No one prompted him, but he managed to pick up the thread on his own. "There ain't no other noise like it. Best one was when I stuck it in a fat Cossack captain . . ."

Dooley had been droning on, rambling from one subject to another without pause, for almost an hour, and for the others in the skimmer, having failed to stop the monologue, it had now become just background noise, like the birds, or Burke's atrocious wind.

"It's not my bloody fault." Their driver admitted responsibility for the most recent succession of rude sounds, after an indignant scowl he'd directed at Dooley had not succeeded in putting the blame for them elsewhere. "These bloody rations do it." He kicked at the litter of wrappers on the floor. "How do they expect a bloke's digestion to work properly on muck like that; plays havoc with my gut."

"Don't do our noses any good either." Jango flapped his hand in front of his face to waft away the smell.

Collins had been watching Dooley as he burnished the bright killing edges of the bayonet. "Shouldn't that be blued, or something, to stop it catching the light?"

"What's the point." Dooley's face creased in another grin as he discovered another pun. "Hey, how's that. I made another joke."

With a sigh of exasperation Cohen paused from resecuring a warped panel on the side of the console. "A clown you may be, a comic you are not. I tell you, if wit were shit you'd be constipated."

Pleased that in Collins at least he had an attentive audience, of sorts, the big man ignored the remark. He turned the weapon over to give it a final buff. "If I ain't using it, it's in here," he patted the sheath, "and when I am using it, I like the Commies to see it coming. Some of them freeze when they see it, makes it easier to stick 'em. So why hide it, and anyway it slides in nice and smooth when it's like this; as well as making that lovely slurping sound as it comes out."

"I thought this was going to be a push-button war."

A loud bellow of laughter from Dooley brought an immediate rebuke from the others, and even he was taken aback at the volume he'd produced.

"Laugh quieter, you fat-arsed crud." Cohen looked at his watch. "Will I be glad when the major gets back, so maybe he can shut you up."

"I kinda get the impression you've amused our lump of lard." Jango had to pound Dooley on the back since he appeared in danger of choking.

"It's a fucking push-button war, or hadn't you noticed." He made a quick recovery.

"Then why are we out here?" Collins was puzzled. "What are we doing with these?" He held up his assault rifle and bag of demolition charges.

"What a fucking innocent." Dooley had his audience back. "I'll tell you how it works. The Heap Big General in Washington, the Pentagon no less, he presses a button on his desk and his aide comes in. The General gives him a three-line order to send out. The aide goes out, presses a lot more buttons and the order goes off. It travels through maybe thirty or forty different command centres and headquarters and the like, and at every stage more buttons are pressed and a load more words get added. Finally it reaches our battalion, only now it ain't three lines, now it looks like the New York telephone directory. Our CO reads the bit that's for him, about sixty pages, and presses a button for our platoon commander. He reads his ten pages and presses a button to send for me. I go charging over, all keen and excited, he looks me into the eye, pokes me in the belly button and says 'attack'."

Dooley sat back, pleased with the effect of his complex recitation, and looked smugly about him in a manner that suggested he was expecting at the very least a standing ovation. All he got was a thundering fart from Burke.

"I'll be glad when this waiting is over, when we know what's going to happen."

"Listen to me, kid." Leaning forward and lightly resting his hand on Collins' knee, Cohen put on his fatherly act. "Enjoy the waiting; to be bored is to be sure you're still alive. It doesn't feature in heaven or hell. As for what's going to happen, the best we can hope for is that we know what is supposed to happen. If we knew what was going to happen, we could cut straight to the end of the war and save a lot of misery."

"I still wish I knew where Hyde and the others were right now."

"You could always ask your friend Clarence." Jango tapped the feet which perpetually shuffled round and round on the gunner's chair.

Since a fighter-bomber had screamed across the tops of the trees at about midday, their stand-in turret gunner had abandoned the Rarden with its limited forty-degree elevation, and manned their anti-aircraft machine gun instead.

"Man, he's gone round so many times he's just got to be in a trance by now. Ask him if he can see into the future."

Collins didn't take up the black's suggestion. Nor did Clarence respond in any way, though Jango had deliberately uttered the words loudly, for his benefit.

"You don't need crystal balls or trances or any of that junk." Between puffs at his cigarette, while watching the large clouds of blue smoke slowly spreading to fill the upper regions of the interior, Dooley had come to the conclusion that here was yet another subject in which he could join. "I know where they are and what's going to happen. I bet you any

140

amount they're in a whore house, they're screwing everything in sight, and we'll get there just in time to be told it's time to be moving on."

"What an imagination." Cohen poured scorn on the big man's prediction. "Those three might well have their hands full, but it won't be of tit and bum. But since you're so sure I'll let you win some of your money back. I'll take you on. Fifty says not one of them has so much as seen, let alone had, a handful of whore. How's that, is that fair?"

There was a loud smack as Dooley crashed his palms together in satisfaction. "You're on, fifty bucks."

"It's a bet." Cohen made a record of the wager in a notebook taken from one of his many pockets. "It's almost a shame to take your money. Does anyone else want to back Dooley's wishful thinking?"

"No way, brother, no way." Rinehart gave up his attempts to administer a drink of water to Nelson. "I know why you wear that armour. I've seen you poke more cash and loot in those pockets than I thought there were in the whole of the Zone. I ain't about to add another bulge to it. Mind you, I'm tempted to take you on. Maybe it's stupid, but I got this hunch that there's just a chance friend Dooley might be right for once. Who knows, maybe he'll even take a few bucks off you yet."

A momentary look of doubt flickered across Cohen's tanned features. It didn't last long. What was he worrying about? Since when had he ever bet on anything other than a sure thing? Dooley already owed him four hundred and fifty, this would make it a nice round number. So maybe he'd never make general, but with a little more luck, god willing, he'd come out of the war with enough cash and goodies to make a three-star's retirement plan look like peanuts. He patted the multitude of flap secured compartments in the flak jacket's front in turn, and checked that each was buttoned down, lingering a little longer over the one with the diamonds in it. That fifty bucks was as good as his already. There was no way Dooley was going to win, no way.

"Sit down. SIT DOWN." Libby shouted at the old scrubber.

With ill grace she plonked back down, turning off the act immediately she was rebuffed, as the three before her had been.

Libby knew what they were up to. They wanted out, the same as the East Germans, and if anything their reasons were stronger. After the attack it wouldn't take the Russians long to figure out who had visited The Farm and, with suspicion and brutality an inbred facet of their nature, they would be sure to turn on the girls. The whores knew that, hence the clumsy, continuous attempts at seduction.

All he had to do was mime his needs and there's be a rush to fulfill them. The thought revolted him. In such a struggle, bound to be heard by the others, he'd have little to say in which of the tarts got to him first, and the older ones with their layers of ill-matched cosmetics and flaccid bodies nauseated him. Old women always made him feel ill. Elderly female relatives had thought him "cold". He had thought them hideous, and had been obliged to force himself to give even the briefest of pecks on cheeks when it had been customarily expected of him on special occasions. Even now, the recollection of that oft repeated and much loathed duty made him cringe.

"I told you to bloody sit down."

This time the woman didn't choose to be cowed so easily. Though she could not have understood the words, their tone and the action that accompanied them had been abundantly clear. The insinuating smile she turned on was complemented by a deliberate loosening of a bow at the neck of her already gaping nightdress. Her body oozed from the threadbare material, and a large brown nipple with hairs sprouting around it was shoved into plain view by the weight of a balloon-like breast.

"I said sit down, get back."

She kept coming, while the others looked on, leaning forward to see what would happen.

A million thoughts, images, emotions flashed in rapid sequence through Libby's mind. Oh God he hated this place, this war, the Zone. Helga, that was all he wanted, just to find her, then none of this would matter any more. He'd desert, go East, West, even stay in the Zone just so long as he could be with her. He needed her, hadn't been with another woman since the war had taken her from him, swept her out of his reach. Frustrations that masturbation had done little to relieve were welling up inside him. All those hours over the last two years spent in finding moments alone and then frantically working himself to a climax.

"You like this?"

A hand was pulling at his trousers, expertly unfastening them, seeking his erection.

"It is wet. You want me?"

143

Waves of sickly sweet perfume filled his nostrils, and through the several layers of clothing he felt the twin hummocks of flesh dangling to the woman's waist rolling against his own stomach. A fat sweat-sticky leg was thrusting between his thighs.

"NO." He hadn't meant the shout to be so loud or the blow so hard.

The pistol pinned between their bodies swept up and the butt of the weapon caught the whore under the chin. Too heavy to be lifted off her feet by the blow, she reeled back, blood from a tooth-pierced bottom lip already staining her naked front, and collapsed among the other women.

"I . . . I . . ." Damn it, he couldn't say he was sorry, he wasn't. "She shouldn't have kept bothering me . . . it was her own fault."

The words were understood, or heard, or were ignored as the others gathered around the victim and helped her to a sitting position. She made no complaint, dabbing at her swelling lip with the inside of the hem of her garment. All of them bore marks and bruises on various parts of their bodies, some on their faces. The elderly whore had had longer than most to get used to the inevitable punishments that went with her trade. Once the bleeding was staunched her concern turned to her fussily trimmed nightdress and she checked it over inch by inch, heedless of how much she exposed herself in the process, until she was satisfied that no outward facing material was marked.

To conceal what he felt sure must be the still huge and obvious mound of his erection, Libby leant in a corner and crossed his hands in front of himself. There was still six hours until last light. It was going to seem a

144

lifetime if he had to stay in here. When the attack commenced time would speed up a hundredfold.

The thought of the fighting didn't worry him, he was certain he'd come through it. God had screwed up his life enough already, the bugger couldn't be so bloody spiteful as to bring it to an end before he found Helga again. Only the Communists practised nastiness of that order.

Libby fished out and threw the woman a bar of chocolate he'd been saving for later. He now regretted having used so much violence, the desired effect could have been achieved by using less, or perhaps none at all. It'd been partly his own fault that the situation had got so far out of hand. Despite himself he'd been fascinated as well as repelled by the sight of the plump body offered him. He pushed the idea from his thoughts, shuddering to physically aid its departure.

Perhaps sometime, not now, it wouldn't hurt just to have one woman. He'd do it very quickly, seeking nothing but swift gratification of a very basic need, Helga would understand, he knew she would. He'd held out so long. Yes, perhaps he would, the present might be easier with that future to think on. And now he had that to look forward to, the afternoon would pass all the sooner and bring the future, and Helga, nearer.

"It's not a lot to go on, Major." Hyde looked at the sketch. The pencilled outline, looking rather like a plump bullet, that was the detached section of the camp in which they were interested bore very few details, and those had question marks against them.

145

"You might as well say it, it's damn-all. We've got the right place. These deep churned tracks leading to it," Revell shaded in a mass of lines that converged on the head of the bullet, "they scream tanks. That area down there that looks like any other piece of the camp is just a shell, outer camouflage for the 97th's workshops, and we can't find out a damned thing about it."

Beads of sweat were trickling down from Hyde's hairline, making glistening lines on the pinkly unreal tissue of his reconstructed face. It was sweltering in the attic. The two tiles they had prised loose and sent skittering down the roof to land with shattering crashes behind the house had done nothing to aid the flow of air, bring any cooling draughts. He took another look out of the hole.

They were only five hundred yards from the place, and with the advantage of a couple of hundred feet of elevation over it, and still apart from the probable location of the main entrance they knew nothing, except that they had been right about the minefield going all the way around. A wide belt of untrampled and rampant grass testified to that.

There was no doubt at all that the workshop was a very juicy target. Packed into those few acres was a battalion that would normally have spread its valuable vehicles and machinery over several times that area to avoid making a concentrated target. Nestling under the wide false roof were engine shops, armouries, assembly lines, machinery trucks, welding bays and masses and masses of stores the Russians could ill afford to lose.

"So what do you think?" The major waited for Hyde to finish his inspection of their target.

"I think we'll need an awful lot of luck to do any real

146

damage if we go at it without knowing which part is which."

"I agree. One of the main problems is that they won't keep much in the way of fuel and ammunition there, those will be in dumps elsewhere, so we can't even hope for a lucky hit on one of those helping us out."

"There is one thing though." A thought suddenly struck Hyde. "The Russians are a sloppy lot of buggers when it comes to safety measures, and I can't believe the 97th will be any different."

"So?" the point eluded Revell.

"So the workshops are accepting tanks straight from the frontline, fuelled and armed. When a tank reaches a REME workshop the first thing that happens is that the ammo is removed. If the Ruskies stay true to form and don't bother, then every tank in there will be better than a one-ton bomb."

"It's a good idea, we go for the tanks as well as the machinery and personnel . . ."

"And if just a few of them brew up and their racks blow, they'll gut the place."

"Very neat, I like it, but we still come back to the fact that we don't know where the tanks, or the machinery or anything is. It's a pity Libby was so fast on the trigger, we could have used those . . ."

"Russians. There are Russians coming." It was Andrea, calling from downstairs.

"How many, and where?" Revell was the first back down.

"Just two." Keeping well back from a yellowed net curtain, she indicated the pair of brown clad, black booted soldiers who were surreptitiously working their way towards the rear of the farmhouse. Their pistols

147

were holstered, and all they carried was a haversack each.

"They're not after us. They're coming to visit their girlfriends." The major watched as the Russians cautiously peered out from behind the cover of a rusting farm tractor at the back door. The nervousness they displayed at every move they made and noise they heard indicated that they were breaking a lot of regulations by being there. "I want them alive, one at least. Andrea, tell Kurt and the others not to fire, not unless a lot more come running, but I think these two are very much on their own. OK, Sergeant Hyde, let's you and me go and prepare a welcome for our visitors."

Masses of half-eaten scraps of food littered the kitchen floor. Hyde slipped and almost fell when his boot skidded on a slice of cucumber, as the two of them took up places of concealment.

They had to wait several more minutes before a shadowy outline showed behind the frosted pane in the door's upper half, and there was a tentative, almost apologetic knock. It was repeated a little louder though still timidly, and then again. Slowly the handle began to turn and the door opened just a crack.

"Sophie?"

The accent was abominably thick, the word only just recognisable as a name. Squeezed into a narrow space between a dresser and a far corner of the room, Revell watched the door gradually open further and a boyish looking junior sergeant hesitantly step into the stone floored room. He clutched the haversack to his chest, and bore a look that suggested if anyone said "boo" to him he'd die of heart failure on the spot. He listened. The absence of an expected reception, and of noises elsewhere in the establishment that might have explained it, obviously puzzled him. A few muttered words were exchanged with the second man, still just outside the door, and then he too came in.

Growing more confident the junior sergeant put his pack down on the table dominating the middle of the room and made a joking remark to his friend, who was quietly closing the door.

Both whirled round as Revell leapt out and Hyde crashed back the door of the storeroom where he'd been hiding. For a second they stared, uncomprehending, at the strange figures that had surprised them, then the last to enter, faster on the up-take or more stupid than his companion, reached for his holster. He never even touched it.

The barrel of Hyde's pistol smacked into the back of his neck and he went down as if pole-axed. His helmet flew off as his face hit the floor sickeningly hard.

Sheer terror, partly from the fright he'd received and partly from the expectation of having the same treatment meted out to himself, had immobilised the young NCO. All colour had drained from his face and he was visibly shaking. Eyes wide, mouth opening and closing soundlessly he raised his hands and clamped them together on top of his helmet without being told. Revell took his pistol.

With the toe of his boot Hyde nudged the head of the man on the floor. It lolled back and forth without any resistance, revealing a sluggishly forming pool of pink bubbled blood. "Broken neck, I didn't think I'd hit him that hard. Must have been when he nose-dived."

He bent down and turned the corpse over to investigate an expanding pool of what looked like

149

water, issuing from the haversack lying partially hidden under the body. Broken glass chinked as he picked up the dripping bag. He caught some of it on his fingers, and tasted it. "Vodka. Looks like they were planning a party."

From the bag on the table he took out two long plump sausages, a loaf, a jar of what appeared to be apricot jam and two more bottles. "Funny, isn't it. Now and again we get Ruskies coming over to us just so they can get a decent meal, what food they get is rotten; but they can always manage to get hold of a little extra when it suits them. They're a crafty lot of buggers, I wouldn't fancy one for a neighbour or workmate."

The surviving Russian swallowed loudly as for the first time he caught a full view of Hyde's horror mask, and he clenched his eyes as if in the hope that the apparition would go away.

"How is your command of Russian, Sergeant?"

"What little there is, rather rusty. Like I said, we haven't taken prisoners in a while."

"Well between us we should be able to cobble a few relevant questions together and understand the answers, if we get any."

Hyde gestured threateningly with his pistol. The junior sergeant's gaze followed every movement. "If we start right away I think the problem will be slowing him down, not getting him to talk."

"Right, so let's get him up to the attic where we won't be disturbed. Time's getting short. And bring the bag. I'm not too keen on that firewater of theirs, but I don't want Kurt's men getting hold of it. They're a big enough risk already."

Browning automatic in one hand, bag of food and

drink in the other, Hyde herded the Russian ahead of him as they followed Revell back to the attic.

They passed Andrea on the way up. Revell noted the taut line of her mouth, accentuating her high cheeks, as she watched the Russian. He wouldn't be putting her in sole charge of their prisoner, certainly not until they'd got what they wanted from him, and possibly not even then. There was cruelty in the lovely face, as much as he had ever seen in any man, and more than in any woman. Seeing her he understood a little more.

It wasn't love or passion or jealousy that would bring animation and intensity into those superb dark brown eyes: hatred might do it, fury could, killing would. She wasn't with Kurt and the other East Germans, they were with her.

Organisation and equipment scales of Soviet 97th Technical Support Battalion.

Commanding officer Major I. V. Pakilev
Officers 27
Men 460
This is regarded among the Soviet forces as an elite unit of its type. All of the officers, and most of the senior sergeants are known to be drawn from the staffs and top graduates of Technical Training Academies in the USSR. All of the personnel are Russian nationals.

Equipment scales for this unit are lavish by Russian standards.
24 ZIL-157 six-wheeled trucks fitted out as mobile workshops.
12 heavy trailers similarly equipped.
2 MAZ-535 eight-wheeled trucks fitted as mobile radar/radio repair shops.
2 ZIL-135 eight-wheeled trucks fitted as mobile cranes. Rated 20 tons.

6 URAL-375 six-wheeled trucks fitted with comprehensive gas and arc welding kits.
3 BTR 50 eight-wheeled armoured personnel carriers converted for medium recovery work.
2 T72 armoured recovery vehicles.
87 other vehicles and trailers.

The 97th is unusual in that it has a light anti-aircraft battery permanently attached for low level air defence. For medium and high level defence it comes under the umbrella of whatever Divison it may be attached to.

Chapter Eleven

The sketch plan of the workshop layout looked a lot more informative now. A mass of detail had been added to it, and while there was no way they could check the veracity of the Russian's answers, if he had made it all up on the spur of the moment he had done a quite remarkable job, the whole dovetailed together very neatly.

Once they had persuaded him to confirm that he was with the 97th the rest had come almost easily, if not eagerly. The junior sergeant was not more than twenty, and it was only his second week in the Zone. This was not something he'd expected to happen to him, and it had taken little persuasion from Hyde for him to forget what seemed at that moment the lesser fear of his superiors and succumb to the aggressive bullying of the hideous Britisher.

"You've missed your vocation, Sergeant." Revell checked the strips of cloth securing their prisoner's arms behind his back. "You should be working as an interrogator with Field Intelligence."

"I've got a job, busting tanks, or I had." Hyde couldn't make up his mind if there was an implied criticism in the comment. "If that load of nut-cases in your G2 want a monster to frighten people with, let them fry one of their own blokes."

Better to let it drop, thought Revell. It had been a stupid mistake he'd not make again. "It's about time you and Libby set off to collect the others. Could take you a good three hours to reach the woods, and you still have to brief them and steal some transport on the way back."

"I'd be a lot quicker travelling on my own."

"We've gone over this already, Sergeant. Both of you go, that way if you run into trouble one of you should still make it. Your aim though should be to collect them and get them back here without causing any sort of ruckus in the process. Unless the Ruskies miss the three guys cluttering the cellar, or our shit-scared comrade here, there's a decent chance they won't have an inkling that we're around until we hit them with all we've got. Make sure you borrow that transport at the last possible moment in case you're spotted or it's missed, and go for the sort of thing Kurt would be tempted by, a supply wagon of some sort. That way if the alarm is raised there's a chance it'll be put down to the refugees, or deserters, and the alert might not spread as far as the workshops."

"I still think we should use the skimmer, Major."

"No." It was a point which he and Hyde had argued at length. "You heard what our helpful Ivan said. Most

156

of the installation is under or behind concrete. That Rarden cannon is good, but not that good. To do the job thoroughly we'll have to work close-in anyway, so its bit of armour will be no advantage. And it could be pretty wild soon after we start. I don't fancy our getaway vehicle getting knocked out by wild strays. If the truck gets hit then we can still hoof it clear and back to the woods. We leave the skimmer where it is."

Hyde had to concede that point, but there was one other he'd already raised, but not got a satisfactory answer to. "What about your wounded man?"

"You mean Nelson?" Revell knew damned well who he meant. "The state he was in when we left, I doubt he's still alive."

, "But what if he is. You want me to leave someone behind to nursemaid him?"

"We need every man we've got for the attack." Hell, this wasn't the sort of thing a man should have to delegate. "You'll have to rig him so he can't harm himself, or attract attention. There's no alternative."

"There is one, and it'd be no harder to do than binding and gagging him while your other men are looking on. I don't think they're going to care for the idea very much. You know them, any suggestions how best to handle them?"

Revell knew what Hyde's option was. It was one that he'd been forced to resort to himself on a deep penetration mission in Yugoslavia that had been loused up, when they'd not been able to bring out two severely wounded men. It was a hard thing to have to do, kneel beside one of your own soldiers and, while his eyes stayed locked on yours, bring your pistol up and

157

administer that single thunderously loud shot to the back of the head, holding the barrel of the automatic an inch from the scalp, just behind the ear. But there was a difference between that, a mercy killing to save a suffering man from the further torments the Russians would inflict, and killing for the sake of convenience.

"Just dose him up and secure him as best you can. Dooley or the others object, tell them it's an order from me."

"I was planning to anyway." Hyde pressed the point he'd made before. "You don't want me to . . ."

"No." Knowing what was coming Revell jumped in. "No, killing Russians is our job. We do that as much and as well as we can. We're soaked in blood enough already without washing in our own."

"If that's the way you want it, Major." He gathered up his few bits and pieces and made ready to leave. "When are you going to tell these GDR thugs what we've got planned?"

"Not till the last possible moment. That way if one of them has ideas about running to the Reds and doing a deal it'll be too late to matter."

"Perhaps they won't be keen on carrying out the part you want them to play." The doubts he'd had from the first about the involvement of the ex-border guards had not deserted Hyde, in fact the very opposite. The whole bunch were traitors several times over. They'd betrayed their country, their people and even their Russian paymasters; and it was a certainty they'd survived in the camp by preying on the weak.

"Don't worry about it, Sergeant. One thing ties them to us, they want out and we can take them. For that reason and no other they'll go along with us in the attack."

"Are we going to take them?" So far Hyde had not been successful in anticipating the officer's answer to any question, or reaction to any situation. More than at any other time he didn't know what to expect now.

"We'll wait." Revell had already given the matter some thought, and the lift capacity of the Iron Cow had not been an important factor. The girl would be going with them, he knew that, had known it from the first moment he saw her. Jesus Christ, why did he have to fall in love with, or want, every woman he met? But Kurt, and the others . . . "We'll wait and see what the casualty list is like."

It was no answer at all, Hyde was fully aware of that. The sequence of action for the assault on the workshop flickered through his mind. Casualties . . . shit, that didn't take much working out. They'd be heavy. Without further comment he left the room and went back down, two stairs at a time, to collect Libby. Now why in hell's name was he hurrying? Casualties . . . yes they'd be high, already were with three-quarters of the platoon destroyed on the way there. That was seventy-five per cent. Everything was bloody decimals or averages or percentages now, and he knew them all: the odds against getting a wound and the percentage that did, point-what of a ton of high explosive had to be dropped to wipe out a platoon. This was a rotten mission, but it would be his last if the percentage figure reached a hundred.

*　　　*　　　*

There was complete silence in the skimmer when Hyde finished the briefing. A long loud fart from Burke was the first thing to break the silence.

"Yeah," Dooley spoke, "that's about the effect it had on me."

"Do any of you have any questions?"

"I have." It was Cohen. "Tell me where the major is holed up at the moment, and what he's doing." He turned an oily self-satisfied smile towards Dooley, and patted his money pocket confidently.

"I've no idea what he's doing, but he's in a place Dooley might like . . . ?"

Cohen's smile began to fade.

". . . It's called The Farm."

With an effort Dooley pulled out the tight waistband of his pants and shouted down into them. "You hear that, you hear where we're going? Great balls of steaming crap, now why can't every fight be like this?" He broke off from addressing his genitals to push away a crumpled scrap of paper Cohen was offering him. "What the hell's that, I want cash, real money."

"It's one of your markers, for fifty bucks; leaves you owing me four hundred."

Dooley looked down into his underwear again. "You just keep on growing, fella, I'll get back to you later." The taut waistband snapped back. "Not so fast, just because you take markers doesn't mean I believe in them. No, I want real money."

A look of mute appeal at the great unreasonableness of the big man's pronouncement met with no sympathy and Cohen put the paper away again. "I don't carry that much."

160

"You lying crud." Jango joined in, enjoying Cohen's annoyance. "In that top left pocket of yours you've got a roll that thick." He waved his bony fist. "Half of it's in twenties, come on, pay the man."

"Shut up, you lot. Sort your debts out after we get back." Hyde grew impatient at the flippancy.

"When you say everyone is going, Sarge," while the bickering had been going on, Burke had given that a lot of consideration, "do you mean *every* one. You know, all of us?"

"All of us." Hyde laid great stress on the "us".

"I'm a driver, not a bloody rifle-man."

"Actually you're a combat driver, so just for once we're going to use the other half of your supposed abilities. You wouldn't have an objection, would you?" Hyde paused only a minute, then injected an aggressive edge into his voice. "Good, you haven't. Right there's work to do," he became brisk. "Libby, take Collins and a roll of tape and mark the safe path to the perimeter of the woods. When we come racing back tonight there isn't going to be time for fancy pussy-footing in the dark."

As the pair departed the sergeant looked around for other work to hand out. Burke and Dooley became instantly engrossed in a minute examination of the nearest objects. In the driver's case it was the fuel gauges. The big man's sudden intense interest in the back of the hand with which he'd been in the act of smothering a yawn was less effective as a task-avoiding ploy.

"You can get working on this lot."

Dooley just caught the satchel of blast grenades.

161

"What do I do with these?"

"I'm sorely tempted to tell you, but what I really want is to have them made up into nice tidy bundles of four or five each. When you've done that, you can do the same with these incendiary grenades."

Comprehension dawned on Dooley, as he accepted a more carefully passed bag of thermite bombs. "Now you're talking business."

Clarence sat at the back of the compartment. Since Hyde and Libby had returned and he'd been summoned down from his position in the turret he'd not said a word; now he looked at Hyde and spoke quietly. "You haven't said precisely what I am doing in all this. Where do I come in?"

Hyde squeezed on to the bench beside the sniper and took out the map. "We'll be taking on the workshops from the direction of the farm, from here, see." He turned the map for Clarence. "Now the Ruskie we collared says there's a pair of camouflaged light anti-aircraft guns on the hill opposite. If they spot us and can get into action, at that range, about a thousand yards, we'll be cut to bits. You'll take up a position on the flank and snipe the crews to pin them down. We'll pick you up on the way out."

There was no concern or emotion in Clarence's voice. "What are they? If they're above machine gun calibre there will be shields for the gun-layers. At that range I'll not be able to get through them, I'll have to content myself with picking off the loaders, and slow their rate of fire."

"All the Ruskie knew was that they were light, only four or five crewmen to each."

162

"Then it'll most likely be twin 23mm or single 57mm mounts. Well, I'll do what I can."

"Good, thanks." Now why the hell had he thanked him. It mildly annoyed Hyde that Clarence always exuded an air of superiority, though there was nothing in his manner, apart from that impeccable accent, that could account for the impression he gave.

Now there was only the wounded man to see to, Hyde had been putting that off. Nelson was still clinging to the last shreds of life. His breathing was starting to become noisy, and every laboured intake seemed like it might be his last, but still the next one came, and the next, and the next.

Rinehart moved over so the sergeant could get a closer look at him.

"He's a tough kid." Hyde almost added "more's the pity", but checked himself. "Do you think he'll last until we get him back?"

"Hey, Sarge, you don't have to have an expression on your face for me to know you ain't really interested. What you want to know is how long is he going to hang on."

"That's what I'm thinking, is it?"

"Sure it is. This ain't the first time I've been in action with the major. He reckons we should pull out all the stops, hit the Commies with all we've got and finish them once and for all. And since he can't get the General Staff to go along with that, he kinda practises it himself. Total War is the term he uses. It sorta fits the way we've always gone about things. Firepower is his God and the Zone is his temple. He wants me up front zapping Reds, not pissing about back here playing nurse. So am I right or am I right?"

"How do you feel about it?" Hyde was conscious that the others were listening.

"What about, killing Reds or leaving Nelson?"

Hyde nodded at the wounded soldier.

There was the briefest hesitation, and the answer was not as slick this time. "We all got to go eventually. Guess he's as comfortable and going as easy as a lot I've seen. Better he kicks the bucket now than lives on with only half a head and no brain. Bed sores, baby food and contempt is all he's got to go back to."

"You ain't thinking of helping the kid along are you?" Dooley paused in his work. "They can fix up most anything now. A guy in 'C' company got scalped by a bomb splinter, took the top off his skull like the lid off a coffee pot. They fitted a plate over the hole and now he's even got hair growing back."

"That was different. Nelson here has lost a chunk of his brain." Peeling back the edge of yet another blood-soaked bandage, Rinehart exposed the scooped-out hollow surrounded by jagged bone and untidy flaps of hair-tufted skin.

The display did nothing to weaken Dooley's stubborn stance. "I'm just telling you, there ain't no one going to give the kid the cut-the-grass. Not while he's in with a chance."

"Who said anything about finishing him? The major just wants us to dose him up and make sure he can't come to any harm while we go off and do the job."

Dooley shifted uneasily. Some of the ground had been knocked from under him, but he wasn't prepared to let it go that easily. "OK, just so long as that's understood. And no trying anything funny like slipping him a couple of extra shots so he OD's."

When the big man had flown off the handle Hyde's immediate reaction had been to regret raising the subject a full hour before they'd have to leave, but now he saw it had worked to his advantage. Dooley would have made the same fuss later on about tying Nelson. By accepting it as a lesser evil, he would presumably raise no further objection when the time came. Now with that out of the way, Hyde began to check off the long list of ordnance they'd be taking with them.

It was impressive, it needed to be, they were going after a very hard target.

"Those friends of yours behaving themselves with the girls?"

Andrea didn't answer the real question Revell had concealed in the sentence. "I do not know, or care. Some of them are keeping a watch, that is all that matters. The whores are used to being abused. It will keep them in practice."

Their Russian captive looked on uncomprehendingly, but constantly glanced from the girl to the officer as they spoke, as though in so doing he might deduce what they were discussing, and whether it concerned him.

"Have you been with Kurt and the others very long?" He tried burying the question another way, determined to find out her relationship with the motley crew of renegades and traitors.

"Why do you not simply ask me if I sleep with them?

165

Are you afraid you will not like my answer?"

"Well, do you?" Her bluntness had surprised him. He tried belatedly to match it.

"No." She added nothing to the bald statement.

Revell probed now that he had at last got her to talk. "What's your secret? One of them must have tried something."

"Yes, one of them did try to have me, when I was first with them. I killed him, before he could. It will save us both time if I tell you I do not like men, so you see there is no use in your pursuing me."

Was he that damned obvious? At one time he'd prided himself on his technique, and he knew it still worked, but not on this one. Apart from a rather mannish middle-aged teacher at high-school, who'd been the cause of much speculation and a host of wild and often absurd or obscene rumours, he'd never knowingly had any contact with lesbians. Was she one? Somehow he couldn't picture her in another woman's arms, but he couldn't picture her in a man's either. She was hard, but she still moved like a woman and could hardly be judged by her appearance. If every girl back in the States who'd ever worn jeans and jacket were a lesbian, then who the hell was it keeping the birth rate up?

"Do you drink?" Revell offered her the opened bottle of vodka, from which both he and Hyde had only taken a sip. It tasted like aviation spirit, and must have been over a hundred proof.

She declined the bottle, but helped herself to the bread, tearing off a piece and dunking it in the jam.

The major considered taking another swig, but

decided against it. He didn't enjoy it that much and to do so might have seemed, would have been, showing off. Christ, he'd thought himself past that stage. It was just that he couldn't find a way through to her. Well, regressing wasn't going to do it. How old was she? Twenty-something or nearer his own age, thirty. There was a frightening maturity about her that many of the most sophisticated women would have striven for years to perfect—and failed. But then the camps were a forcing ground, thrusting people through the spectrum of their adult lives in months rather than years.

"I want you to stay back when we go into action. Kurt and the others will be enough. We can pick you up after."

She went on eating.

"You understand?"

"Yes, I understand." Andrea finished a last mouthful and wiped a sticky orange-coloured blob from the side of her mouth. "It is you who does not understand. You will have much to explain to Kurt about what you want done. If I am not to come, then I shall not translate. I do not think your German is good enough for it, not for all that must be arranged just so."

There was nothing he could say to that, and the girl took his silence as the answer she'd wanted and expected. Now she would be going into action with them.

"I'm going to look at that car, come with me." He'd seen the look she gave their prisoner, that was why he'd added the rider.

The Russian had seen it as well and he started to shake again. A puddle grew beneath him. Although still frightened he had been adjusting to his circumstances, now that one glance reduced him to a state not unlike the one he'd been in minutes after the action in the kitchen.

In the man's place Revell realised he might well have felt the same. He'd never known anybody with the girl's capacity for conveying an emotion or intention with a single look. The Russian had reacted as he might have done to a knife being put at his throat. Revell had caught only a reflection, but it had made the hairs on the back of his neck prickle.

It occurred to him that he had witnessed a more controlled version of the same thing only recently, recalling the incident between Dooley and Clarence. Perhaps he could manage to keep the girl out of the worst of the fighting by pairing her with Clarence. They would make a frightening team.

As he followed her downstairs, the door to the room holding the women was partially open. Grunts, and what sounded like wet bodies slapping together came from it. The glimpse of the filthy bed revealed Kurt, naked from the waist down with his face buried between one woman's jiggling breasts, both of them sitting astride a second tart who was receiving the thrusting force of the East German's runty body, while her own fat chest was crushed by the ample stretch-mark decorated rump of her fellow whore.

Andrea showed no interest, passed by without looking, but not without comment.

"He is a fool, and so are the others who wait their turn. Every one they have will drain that much strength from them, strength they will need." A slight extending of the line of her mouth and a fractional deepening of the fine lines at the side of her eyes might have been an indication of humour, but the venom in her words negated it. "Later they will pay for those whores' bodies with their lives when they cannot keep up. It will be the highest price they have ever paid."

Chapter Twelve

Nelson did not have to suffer the final indignity of being trussed and gagged. As Hyde pulled back the blood-stained sleeve for Rinehart to administer the injection, he felt the growing coolness of the flesh. He let the arm drop. "About ten minutes ago, I should imagine, when we were busy working out how much we could carry."

Dooley heard but there was no reaction from him.

"What's up, aren't you going to rush him away for a burial service?" After the earlier fuss, Hyde was expecting something from the big man.

"He's dead, ain't he? Stick him outside, we're gonna need the room."

"You are not the most consistent person I have ever known."

"So what's it to fucking you, you stuck-up Limey shit," Dooley was very fast rounding on Clarence, not letting the remark go. "I make my own fucking rules: first I look after number one, that's me, then I look after any guy who I reckon is alright, so long as that don't screw up number one, and three I push out of my mind and out of my way anyone who don't feature in one or two because he's either a Commie, or he's not my buddy or he's dead."

"You make life and death sound so simple."

"It is, except for clever arses the like of you. Life is fucking simple: I eat, I drink, I screw and I go to the john. For me happiness is a stiff cock, a full belly and efficient bowels. That covers it all; you want to make it harder than that for yourself then go ahead."

"That still leaves us with a corpse. Burke, Dooley, get him out."

The order was greeted by their driver's ritual protest. "Hey, Sarge. It's bad enough you're dragging me along on this suicide mission, without putting me on burial detail just before the off. I don't fancy doing a spot of digging out there, it's a bloody minefield, or hadn't you noticed?"

"A safe lane has been taped. Take your packs and weapons with you. Dump him where we won't trip over him and then go on to the wire and keep a look out. We'll join you there as soon as the Iron Cow has been booby-trapped."

Burke took Nelson's feet and between them the two men, hampered by their slung weapons and bulky loads, manoeuvred the corpse out on to the ramp, where they paused before getting off to follow the twin pale yellow strips that marked an eighteen-inch-wide lane disappearing into the trees.

"You tell that kid to mind what he's bloody doing." Burke got in a final grouse, as he looked back and saw Collins rigging the five-pound thermite charge that would destroy the skimmer if a Russian patrol should stumble upon it before their return. "He may have been on all the bloody courses and thinks he knows how to handle those things, but just you tell him to be fucking careful. I don't fancy coming back and ending up a charred crisp in a puddle of molten aluminum."

Laden with the body in addition to their load of weaponry, they had to constantly pause to check the positioning of their feet on the snaking ribbon of unmined ground.

"This'll do." Dooley carefully lowered the corpse. The bandage about its head had slipped off, and a broad smear of glistening red, flecked with spongy white, decorated the front of his camouflage suit. "Oh shit, I had this laundered only a couple of months back. Let's have a look at what's around before we shove him out of the way."

Taking out his bayonet, he gently probed at the rank grass and nettles.

"Here, be careful." Backing off a couple of paces Burke watched the operation anxiously. "That stuff was laid nearly two years ago. It could be a bit touchy by now."

"Why in fuck's name don't they set 'em all to self-destruct after a while." Very gingerly Dooley parted the undergrowth, to reveal as a length of bough the object he'd encountered with the probe. "There's bloody choppers buzzing about all over scattering these things. Christ knows how many have been laid by hand and machine, must run into millions. Soon as the Ruskies find them they either bomb 'em or plough 'em up and clear a way through in next to no time."

"Not always." The Russian BMP tracked personnel carrier was almost close enough for Burke to reach out and touch. Two of its road-wheels had been blown off, and there was a gaping hole in its raked frontal armour. It sat amid the curled remains of its tracks, heavily rusted where flames and heat had peeled away its paint. "They still come charging on sometimes."

"Pity a few more don't do it, save us having to tackle so many that get through." Dooley got to his feet. "Yeah, this'll do." With his foot he started the body rolling.

Burke helped move it off the track with similar assistance. "I know one thing, I'm bloody glad it's a skimmer I drive, and not a ruddy tracked APC. With the number of bloody mines the Russians are starting to use, I want as little contact with the ground as possible."

"Less maintenance on one of them as well, ain't there."

A grin spread across Burke's face. It matched Dooley's. "Do you know, I hadn't thought of that but now you come to mention it, you're right."

The shadows, where individual ones could be distinguished beneath the canopy of leaves, were lengthening, though the sun was still a couple of hours from meeting the horizon. The two men had to take care not to touch, or even brush any of the overhanging trees. Many of them bore signs that the explosive devices set among their dangling branches had already detonated. Some of the damaged trunks and shattered stumps were obviously old, dating back to the first fierce battle; but others were more recent, evidence that with age the devices were becoming unstable, capable of being triggered by nothing more than inclement weather. It would be a deadly place to shelter during a storm. Enough of the mines remained to ensure that the threat they posed would exist for a long time to come.

"We can see as much from here as we will out there." Stopping just within the fringe of the trees, Dooley squatted down and looked out over the barbed wire to the rolling farmland.

"No point in taking risks we don't have to," Burke agreed. "We'll be doing enough of that later."

"That's for sure."

"You don't sound too bothered."

"Can't say I am. I reckon when your number's up, it's up, ain't nothing you can do about it." The packet of cigarettes Dooley had half withdrawn from his pocket he crushed back in. "Don't suppose I ought look for trouble though by sending up smoke signals."

"I should think it'd hardly matter, the size of the smoke cloud we'll be creating later. What do you think about this plan of the major's?"

"It's OK, 'cept we're a bit thin on the ground for taking on a battalion of Ruskies, even if they ain't expecting us and are more likely to be holding spanners than AKMs when we hit 'em."

"We'll have to scare the shit out of them to make them keep their heads down for as long as possible, but it'll only be a couple of minutes at most." Burke unslung his pack and sat on it.

"Better jump up a bit sharp if you think you're gonna fart again. You'll lose more than your balls if what you've got in there goes off." Dooley ticked off the contents of Burke's pack to himself. There was enough explosives in it to reduce both of them to lots of tiny pieces and clear a wide area of the woods of mines, and trees. He didn't drop his own load. It was not that he was unaware of the weight of the case of single-shot flames tubes, though at more than eighty pounds it was a load that would have crushed most men, rather that in his opinion to have done so would have tarnished his hard-man image. That was his most prized possession, and one he guarded jealously, nurturing it with ostentatious exercising at every opportunity.

"The others are taking their time." Burke changed the subject.

Dooley just grunted, and went on staring out at the overgrown fields and untended hedges. He wasn't seeing them though, and he hadn't really heard Burke. What filled his mind was the fight to come, he could picture it, and his part, as clearly as if he were watching it on a screen. Rows of yelling, charging Russians fell before him, tens, hundreds of them and still they kept coming and still he kept firing; he was spreading destruction all about him. He didn't feel the wounds, felt no sense of danger. Another scene swam into his mind and swamped the first; the White House lawn, a special ceremony: there were cameras, reporters, private words from the President, a shining medal on a cushion . . .

"On your feet, this is no time for bloody dreaming."

Hyde's words dissolved the fantasy, and once more Dooley saw the fields. He rose to his feet, deliberately doing it the hard way, not giving himself a push with his hands.

"We'll move out in small groups of twos and threes, strung out but not too far apart." There was no need for Hyde to raise his voice to be heard by the men tailing back along the path. No other sound disturbed the still woods. "Keep in sight of each other at all times. We're only going as far as the first track or road that looks like it's used regularly by heavy Russian traffic. The Commies are supposed to move only by night, but I'm counting on there being a few idiots who start out early. With any luck one of them will come our way and we'll be able to collar transport before the rush builds up and it becomes impossible."

"What about refugees. How do we handle them if we're spotted?"

Hyde recognised Libby's voice from the back of the line.

"I don't think that'll be a problem. It's not long to curfew. If there are any about who are cutting it a bit fine, they'll be in such a bloody hurry to get home they won't even notice us."

"What kinda transport we looking for, Sarge?" It was Rinehart who raised the issue.

"Well, it's got to hold all of us, plus the major and his new recruits, that consideration apart, anything, anything at all."

Dust raised by the speeding Gaz scout car settled on the men crouched behind the hedge. Dooley spat out mouthfuls of grit and made repulsive noises as he blew his nose.

"Do you have to do that?" Clarence wiped his tongue with a handkerchief.

"What are you beefing about? One good spit is better than what you're doing. For fuck's sake quit it; dragging that dry rag around your mouth is worse than scraping your fingernails down a blackboard."

Cohen ignored the exchange as he turned to Hyde. "That's the third vehicle in twenty minutes to pass us like there was a race on. How do we stop one of those without breaking it?"

"We don't. We'll stop the next one anyway we can, then go back into hiding and wait for the following vehicle crew to stop and help whoever we clobber." Hyde beckoned Clarence over. "Take out the driver. Don't worry about the noise. It'll be nothing to the crate going over."

"Where do you want it to land?"

"I'll be happy as long as it's on the road and not on us."

Without any further discussion Clarence departed to set up his ambush. A moment later he had melted into the countryside. There was a five-minute wait before the next Soviet army vehicle came along.

It was a Toyota pick-up, one of the mass of civilian vehicles the Russian forces had pressed into use when the war had begun to extend beyond the time they had planned, and they'd had to return their own called-up supply trucks to the dislocated civilian economies of East Germany and Poland. This one was a battered and sorry example: dents and scrapes that marred every panel exposed large areas of its original bright-red paintwork, showing startlingly vivid against the thin coat of olive-drab still adhering elsewhere.

Through his glasses Hyde watched the pick-up's fast approach. He could just, through the layer of dust on its screen, make out the pale blob of the driver's face. "Looks like it's the boy racers who come out early, taking advantage of clear roads and no traffic police." Occasionally the Toyota would jink to the side, as its

178

driver slung it around the worst of the many pot-holes.

There was a distinctive double click as Libby cocked his rifle. "I hope Clarence is going to hit him soon, or we'll have the perisher landing in our laps."

As it came nearer, filling his field of vision, Hyde found it more difficult to follow the progress of the bucking vehicle, but he had a perfect view of it at the precise moment the sniper's single bullet shattered the windscreen.

Fired from close range the 7.62mm round drilled through the driver's right temple and clean through his head, emerging behind his left ear in an eruption of flesh and bone fragments as the tumbling deformed bullet gave up the last of its energy.

For another fifty yards the pick-up held course, then collision with the steep side of a deep pot-hole jerked the steering to the right and it struck the shallow bank flanking the track. There was a geyser of dirt and dust as the vehicle impacted. It rose up as though launched from a ramp, displaying the crumpled front end, trailing steam from its crushed radiator. The short flight ended in a nose-dive back on to the road. Both front wheels jammed up under the bodywork, it slewed to a final halt rocking on what was left of its suspension, straddling the track and surrounded by a litter of unidentifiable components. A bloodied arm hung from a window and the air was thick with the stink of petrol fumes and clouded with a shroud of steam. One oval wheel spun lazily in the road, a hub and stub axle still attached to it.

The wreck had eventually come to a halt only a few yards from where the men lay.

"That sodding mad-arse cut it a bit fine."

179

"One yard or fifty, Burke." Hyde heard the complaint. "What does it matter? He gets the job done, that's the main thing."

Burke couldn't win, and he knew it. His past provided too much ammunition for the sergeant for it to be of any use arguing with him. Besides, what bloody private ever won a real argument with a sergeant?

"Dooley, Rinehart, you take out the crew of whatever stops at this roadblock. Use your knives. Take your time and let them get well clear of their vehicle first."

Rinehart weighed the sergeant's instructions. "Now just what if the first truck along happens to be packed full of infantry. How you expect us to deal with that?"

"I don't and you won't have to, we'll be covering you."

"Well give me time to get back in the fucking ditch before you open up." Dooley took out his bayonet and lightly ran his thumb down the edge of the double-sided blade. "Which side of the road do you want?"

"I'm comfy here, how about you taking the stroll?" As though it were the most elegant of toppers, Rinehart tipped his helmet rakishly over one eye and twirled a non-regulation leather-handled, saw-backed Bowie knife.

Affecting a casual air Dooley left the hedge and strolled over to the far side, pausing on the way to shake the hand hanging limply from the Toyota. He glanced back to see if his act was being appreciated before ducking out of sight.

"Bloody clown."

"Bloody good one though, Sarge." It had taken an effort by Libby not to gratify the big oaf by laughing out loud.

"I don't have any use for a funny man, this is the Zone, not a three-ring circus."

Having saved Collins from trouble by nudging him hard to shut up his giggling before Hyde found some other way of doing it, Cohen sidled over to the sergeant. "A silly bastard at times he may be, but there's a lot of Commies who don't think so, come to that they don't think any more at all."

"I'll believe that when I see evidence of it for myself."

"Here's your chance." Fastening his body-armour tighter about himself, Cohen went back to his place.

It wasn't in sight yet, but the throaty low revving rumble of an approaching truck was very clear in the still evening air. Clarence, further along the road and able to see more of the track, briefly put in an appearance and held up two fingers.

No order was given, no man looked to another, but as though at a signal all of them slipped off their packs and reached for their knives.

Cohen patted Collins' arm. "Stick with me. This is where it starts to get messy."

Major Revell had already been over to a front window twice, and now he found himself there for the third time, looking down the long winding track leading to the farm.

They would not have the light for much longer, and the hollow among the hills holding the workshops would be the first to lose the sun. Already a band of shadow was starting down from the crest of the rise partly hiding it from the farm. In an hour it would be like the night down there.

The sinking bloated orange ball was shining directly in through the window, almost blindingly bright. It was very quiet. Even the whores in the adjoining room were silent. Kurt and his men had finished their "turns". Andrea was in there now, guarding the women.

The regular patrons were not expected until after sunset, and Revell could only hope that none of them, like the officers Libby had killed, and the two junior sergeants, would try queue-jumping.

He had spent most of the afternoon observing the workshops. There had been no vehicle movement anywhere in their vicinity, and with only the surrounding ground to study he had come to know every inch of it, picking the route they would take and the best spot for their sniper. After repeated examinations of the far slopes he'd even tentatively identified the position of one of the flak guns their prisoner had mentioned.

The Russian was still lying bound in the loft. At first Revell had called Andrea at every impassioned outburst from the soldier and tried to make out what it was he was so urgently trying to tell them. On the fifth repetition of his conversion and devotion to the capitalist system and his earnest intention to desert to the West, Revell had gagged him with his own belt.

There was no way, with his limited command of the language, that Revell could determine whether or not the soldier was genuine, or opportunist. A lot of men had deserted from the Soviet forces, a few still managed to do so, but the numbers had fallen drastically since the Communists had instituted a system that relied on brutal reprisal for its effectiveness. Those who came over from Russian units were

182

mostly Armenians, Estonians, Turkomans; single men without family ties, who didn't care what happened to the men of the units they deserted. That was an ironic result of the deliberate Communist policy of splitting up the various ethnic and national groups, so that men from the far reaches of the Soviet territory, speaking hardly any Russian, would find themselves thrown among others with whom they had nothing in common, not even language.

Each time Revell thought he had seen every last repugnant facet of Communism he discovered a new one, and it was always uglier, nastier, more calculated than the previous ones.

A large portion of that nastiness would come their way if they were caught. The various conventions of war had been thrown out of the window by the Soviets. While they screamed at any hint of the West ignoring them, they flouted any it suited them to, and most of the time that was all of them. Better by far to go down fighting, take some of them with you, than fall into their hands alive.

The noise of approaching engines broke into his thoughts.

Engines! Hell, that wasn't right. Hyde was supposed to be bringing only one vehicle, if he could. Turning into the lane was a Russian command car, and behind it a six-wheeled tilt-rigged Ural truck. Two hundred yards away both halted, and heavily armed men began to jump from the transport.

Chapter Thirteen

"Five seconds more and I'd have told Kurt and his cut-throats to open up on you. It was only because I saw Dooley . . ."

The two captured vehicles had been driven up to the farmhouse, and Revell had just finished inspecting them.

"We came up on the place before I was expecting it. I realised what you might think when you saw two wagons coming, so I had the men de-buss in case you started popping off." Hyde patted the roof of the utility-bodied command car. "We cut three Commie throats to get these, so I thought we might as well use them both. What do you think, Major?"

"Oh, I think we can find a use for them both. Let's get inside." Revell led the way. "I'll brief the Grepos now. Have two men relieve Andrea and tell her to bring Kurt and the others to the kitchen. We have to move fast before we lose the light."

Only Burke and Dooley were available, all the others were busily engaged in checking and setting up the weapons in the six-wheeler.

"Just remember, you two. We're moving out in a matter of minutes, don't start anything. I don't want to shout and have you trot down the stairs with your tongues out and your pants round your knees. Have you got that, do I make myself clear?"

"Very loud, extremely clear, Sarge."

"And you as well, Dooley."

"Sergeant Hyde, sir. I hear every word. I promise not to let them seduce me. I shall also keep a tight hold on my weapon."

"Funny man." Misgivings flooded over Hyde, but there wasn't the time to change the arrangements. "Follow me." Two steps up the stairs he stopped abruptly. "Dooley, you step on my bloody heels once more, just once more . . ."

"That one, I think." Dooley stuck his hand down the front of his pants and unashamedly rearranged his rapidly expanding self. The object of his attention did not reciprocate his interest, she yawned.

"Oh fuck me . . ."

"No thanks." Burke declined the invitation.

". . . look at them, have you ever seen such a wanked-out bunch of old hags in all your life."

"Not all at once, no."

Becoming impatient Dooley crossed to the women. They all avoided his eye, and his attempts to pull one of them from the herd. "How about you, you fancy a quick one?" He addressed the remark to the youngest, she shook her head. The words hadn't meant anything, but the question was a familiar one and she understood his tone.

"Shit. I don't bloody believe it." Dooley pounded his fist into the crumbling plaster on the wall, and left a row of indents. "I'm in a brothel, a real live fucking brothel, and all the tarts are on strike. Bloody hell, the sodding unions are killing everything." He grew desperate. "Come on, one of you, any of you." From various pockets he extracted all his worldly goods; two packets of cigarettes, twenty marks, mostly in change, and a cheap lighter. "You can have all this." Again the fist battered at the fabric of the building.

Burke scanned the women. They looked terrible. He'd seen rough before, but not like this. "Back off, mate. You're better not poking one of these, look at them, they're red-raw." He indicated a middle-aged individual who was slouched in such a way, with one foot tucked partially under her, that she was completely exposed. "What this lot need is a jar of vaseline, not another cock."

"I'll skin the major. Why'd he let those scabby GDR cruds have a go. They've screwed it up for us."

"For you, you mean. I'm not touching one of them. The Ruskies don't have them inspected regular like we do. I bet you there's more pox to the square fanny in this room than anywhere else in the whole of the Zone."

"I'd have risked it, whatever shape their fannies were. Did you see that piece with the major? She's not with this mob."

"I saw her." Burke was glad the conversation was changing tack, even if only slightly. "Nice, if you like them hard. She looked the sort that if you woke up beside her in the morning, the first thing you'd do

187

would be to check she hadn't bitten your balls off in the night."

A low growl escaped from Dooley. "Christ, what I wouldn't give for something like that."

"Not a chance for the likes of us, maybe not for the major either. She's something special. I don't know what sort of bloke she'd go for, but he'd have to be at least as hard as her."

"OK, you two." Revell put his head around the door. "Herd this lot downstairs and stay with them. Keep them out of trouble, and keep them out of the way."

"What are we going to do with them, Major?"

"We're letting them go, Burke. If we leave them here the Russians will practise nastiness on them; but if they scatter into the camps they'll never be found." With that he was gone, clattering back down the stairs and out to the truck.

"They'll get a hell of a reception in the camp if they're dressed like this." Lots of bare flesh bulged at Burke from every quarter. "You hang on here. I'll find their rags."

As the door closed behind Burke, Dooley sighed his contempt and frustration. "Useless bloody lot. You wouldn't know a good cock if you saw one. Move over, you scabby cows, I want to sit down."

The filthy lumpy mattress felt good after hours on the thinly padded bench in the skimmer. As the whores parted to make room for him a large warm breast brushed his arm and smooth satin rustled.

"All I wanted was a bloody good fuck." Absently his hand went out to the nearest backside and slid beneath it. His forefinger played in the fabric covered crevasse. A hand landed on his knee and began to slide up his thigh. Other hands came at him, and he just sat there. "It's no good, you're wasting your time. You're too late by five minutes and eight inches."

The door flew open and an avalanche of variously coloured clothes and underwear preceded Burke's return. "Hello there. You look like you're nicely settled."

"No way. At this moment I couldn't stuff a shitty olive. Marvellous, ain't it." Pushing aside the hands that sought to hold him back, Dooley got up and walked to the pile. "Here, come and get this lot on."

There was a mad scramble as the women fought to salvage their own things and steal all they could of everyone else's. Dooley had to put his large boot to several similarly dimensioned behinds before he succeeded in reducing the row they were making.

Burke was repulsed rather than sexually aroused by the sight of the fighting women. Huge rumps, bobbling breasts, all were on show in abundance and had no effect on him.

The major shouted from downstairs and the two men began to propel the women along the corridor while they were still fumbling, hopping and contorting to finish dressing.

"No one would ever believe this." His erection had completed disappeared. Dooley knew it without checking. "I ain't never gonna tell anyone about this, not ever. I spend fifteen minutes in a brothel; the first five I'm trying to grab a broad, the next five I'm trying to keep a load of whores from finding out that I'm not all I'd like to be and was five minutes before, and the last five I'm forcing them to get dressed and chucking them out. I just don't like myself at the moment. Maybe in a year I'll have forgotten all about it; the hell I will."

Andrea was coming down the stairs.

"There you are." Revell steered her to the women. "Tell them to get down to the camp and lose themselves, and don't take no for an answer. I want them out right now."

He started up the stairs. In a crazy way he'd be doing the Russian a favour. If the Soviet security services got him to tell the whole story, and they would, including how he had given the enemy an inch-by-inch description of the workshops, then the last few hours of his life would be very painful and unpleasant.

Cradling the 12 gauge assault-rifle Hyde had brought him from the skimmer, he climbed to the top of the building. It would be best if he fired right away, from the door of the attic: no need to make a ceremony of it. He paused at the door, laid the heavy twenty-shot weapon on the floor and took out his pistol. The weight of the silencer unbalanced the Colt and he had to consciously counteract it.

As he put his hand to the door, he paused again, and checked that the safety catch was off. The air held a smell he hadn't noticed before, like, like overdone meat. Dismissing it from his mind he pushed open the door.

Thick grey smoke filled the room, drifting in layers in the warm, still air. Wisps of it wafted out through the hole in the roof. The smell was much stronger now, almost overpowering. He felt his way to the wall and began to work his way round the room. In a far corner

190

he discovered a smouldering bundle. It was the Russian. Blue and yellow flame still rippled through his hair and what was left of his uniform. Two empty vodka bottles lay nearby.

Revell did not make a close examination, pumping two shots into the man to extinguish any last vestige of life. At the impact, sparks and clouds of black particles flew up and he had to step back smartly to avoid them settling on him.

The body lolled sideways, scraping off long ribbons of red-streaked black tissue on the wall. Smoke from the still smouldering belt about the lower half of what had been a face, found its way out through the misshapen holes in the charred remains of a nose.

In two years of savage war in the Zone, the deliberate incineration of a bound and helpless prisoner was as inhuman an act as Revell had ever witnessed. It was almost the equal of the worst atrocities the Russians had committed.

He knew: he had no proof, but he knew who had done it. What had happened to Andrea, what could she have been through to turn into a person capable of this? It went far beyond anything that the motives of revenge or hate could justify.

Now there was no question of leaving her with Clarence when the attack went in. He would keep her with him and though that might make him uneasy, he was not unhappy at the prospect. If there was more in her than the urge to kill then he wanted to know, find out how to get past or through that tough shell she presented to the world. It would be no easier or safer than the job they were about to tackle.

Hyde was calling him. The men were ready for the final briefing. It was almost time.

The major connected the last wire of the intricate layout of booby-traps that Burke had set about the house, then carefully closed the front door before climbing into the command car. Burke already had the engine turning over smoothly.

Andrea sat between Revell and the driver. Four of the Grepos crouched on the floor in the back, still wearing the same dull sullen expressions the officer had first noticed at Mother Knoke's. They had not altered in all those hours, save for the brief strained grimaces while they'd been with the women.

"Damn it." Revell swore. "We didn't rig that Merc."

"Collins took care of it." Burke slowed the car after passing out of the farmyard, while he waited for Hyde, piloting the big truck, to negotiate the narrow opening. "It'll go bang at the same time as the house, or maybe it'll be the other way round. Either way, any sloppy Commies are in for a hell of a fucking shock."

There was a lurch as the car left the track and then the vehicle's four-wheel drive was pulling them effortlessly towards the top of the hill. The sun was still a few minutes from the horizon and sent the car's long shadow ahead of it to the crest.

"Take it easy as we go over, then head to your left so we hit the main approach track about three hundred yards from the entrance." Scouring the floor of the hollow time and again, Revell searched for other traffic. It was early yet, but as the Ural topped the rise behind them he spotted something. A lone T72 was heading in the same direction.

"OK, stop here. Give Sergeant Hyde the signal." As Burke lowered the window and waved, Revell turned in his seat to watch Clarence jump from the back of the truck and then take the bulky packs handed to him.

Hyde had seen the Russian main battle tank as well, and noted that it was travelling opened up with its two-man turret crew sitting half out of the roof hatches. Dust and thick white exhaust smoke plumed out behind it.

"Looks nice and quiet down there." Libby had to hold tight as they reached the bottom of the slope and Hyde wrenched the wheel over to turn on to the track a hundred yards behind the tank, keeping only a length between themselves and the command car in front. "Those tank blokes wouldn't be so casual if they thought there was any trouble in these parts."

"Very likely, but I think we've got trouble. There's something up ahead, at the gap in the minefield where the track goes through. Looks like a traffic control point."

Libby unclipped a grenade from his webbing and rested it in his lap. A lone military policeman stood beside the track. Two motorcycles were parked beside a small tent, half-hidden by a movable barbed wire barricade that was pulled back out of the way.

The MP waved the tank through, then saw the command car approaching and stepped out into the road to flag it down.

With a noisy grinding of gears Hyde changed down as the lead vehicle slowed. "Why in fuck's name is he doing that? He let the tank through."

"Perhaps we should be showing lights, or maybe

these wagons shouldn't be here at all." Libby watched the command car. At a couple of lengths from the Russian it had almost slowed to a stop, then with a bellow of its exhaust it surged towards him.

His shouting unheard above the roar of the engine the MP jumped back, starting to unsling his AKM as he did so. The car almost brushed him and, as the passenger window drew level, he suddenly clutched at his chest, staggered and crumpled.

"There's another of the bastards."

In response to Libby's yell Hyde slung the wheel hard over, stamped on the gas pedal and hurled the big wagon straight at the second MP who was scrambling from the little tent, pushing his rifle before him.

If the Russian screamed he wasn't heard. The deep treaded tyres crushed him into the hard earth and the tent was ripped to shreds by the tangled mass of barbed wire and broken stakes the truck bulldozed before it.

As Hyde hauled the encumbered vehicle back on to course, a wheel ran over the parked motorcycles and the wire was dragged from the truck as it straightened up again behind the command car.

Ahead of them the track led right up to the camp. Burke had seen the tank drive into the motley collection of shelters and appear to melt away. For a moment he had the wildly illogical thought that he'd follow it and find it had crushed a bloody course over hundreds of refugees.

"Keep going." It was hardly noticeable, but Revell's senses were tuned to such a pitch that he instantly noticed the tiny check to their speed. "Follow the tank."

What, from his vantage point up in the roof of the farm, had looked like the start of just another of the many paths that wound through the camp, as they got closer revealed itself to be wide enough to comfortably accept the car, and the truck behind it.

Immediately it started to slope steeply and, as it levelled out again, the false roofs of the camp were forty feet above them, supported by lattice girdering. It was a very different view to the one from outside.

"I'll have to put the side lights on, I can't see a sodding thing." Fumbling about with the unfamiliar controls, Burke managed to turn on the wipers and interior light before he pulled the correct knob. He found it just in time.

The faint illumination they provided showed a curtain of what looked like thick black canvas blocking their way.

"It's just a black-out screen." Revell punched Burke on the arm. "We're committed now, drive on." He brought up his combat shotgun and levelled it out of the window. Six more of the big twenty round drum magazines were attached to his belt, another lay in his lap. "Just take it slow, don't lose contact with the truck."

Burke shoved the gear lever across and down, and they began to nudge forward into pitch darkness. The coarse material parted in the middle and scraped and flapped down either side of the car, then slapped together behind them.

The six-wheeler was halfway through the first curtain when the car reached a second, twenty yards ahead. Cohen, riding in the back of the Ural, heard the frayed edge of the material as it brushed along the steel hooped canvas top. He'd rejected the small window of smoked perspex in the tilt and was looking out of the weapon slit he'd made below it. There was nothing to be seen in the inky blackness.

Dooley had a better vantage point, looking forward, over the truck's cab roof. "I can see the car's lights, looks like there's another of these doors, he's driving into it now . . . Jesus Christ."

A blaze of white light, a blast of noise and roasting hot air burst over them.

Clarence watched both vehicles until they disappeared from sight, and then began to assemble the tripod supporting the high powered night-sight. The light was failing fast now, though the sky was still a uniform mid-blue, tinged in places with speckles of reddish-brown, a trace of the contamination spreading out from the centre of the Zone.

He brought his attention back to earth, to the dark slopes of the far hills. There was nothing to be seen with the naked eye, nor with the pocket image intensifier he tried. Its definition was poor compared with the larger ones aboard the skimmer, but it was good enough to confirm that what he sought lay under heavy camouflage.

It was already noticeably cooler now that the sun had gone down, there was even a suggestion of a breeze ruffling the grass. Clarence loosened the locking nut on the tripod, sat behind the sighting unit and panned along the hillsides. Near the top of one almost opposite, some eleven hundred yards away, he saw what he'd been expecting to find. It didn't look much,

196

but the infra-red view showed a patch of distinctly colder ground.

"Got you, you ugly bastards."

The second anti-aircraft position wasn't so immediately obvious, but he knew it would show up soon. Several layers of camouflage netting offered some cover in the daytime, but at night they gave up their small amount of stored heat very rapidly, and the ground below them, in the shade all day, quickly showed up against the still warm surrounding open slopes.

From the direction of the workshops came the dull boom of an explosion. Clarence ignored it and went on with his survey; he was looking for targets of his own.

Chapter Fourteen

Andrea threw her arms across her face to shield her eyes. After the pitch black of the entrance ramp, the glare from the arc lights set in the high roof of the workshop complex was intense. She felt Revell lunge past her and grab at the wheel.

Quickly recovering from the temporary blinding, Burke brushed aside the officer's hands and made the sharp left turn himself. He hardly needed to remember the layout of the place, he held a map of it in his hands; the steering wheel rim was the perimeter road, the four spokes the radial service lanes, and the boss the massive bunker of reinforced concrete that held the main tank repair facilities. He caught a glimpse of it over the top of intervening blast walls and stacks of crated spares.

The total area was vast, like four gigantic hangars sunk together into the ground, and high overhead a web of steel supported the artificial roof of the refugee camp.

They drove almost immediately into what looked like a reception and dispatch area. Ten or eleven main battle tanks were parked close together, mostly T72s and the latest T84s, with a couple of elderly T62s, both fitted with heavy mortars and bulldozer blades for demolition work. A swarm of fitters was working on them, attaching or removing auxillary fuel tanks, infra-red searchlights and anti-aircraft machine guns. Close by, two Russian officers discussed details on an engineering drawing. They did a double-take as the command car drew level with them, and died. A burst of five rounds from Revell's automatic shotgun cut both down, and tumbled three fitters from the T72 behind them.

Hyde didn't hear the firing above the din of generators and machinery that filled the place, but he saw the victims go down, and anticipating the car's increase in speed, put his foot to the floor.

Fire from the automatic weapons aboard the car and truck hosed the fitters from the tanks and smashed every unarmoured fitting on them. From the back of the truck, Collins and Rinehart lobbed thermite grenades at each AFV in turn. A few rolled from the armour, but most came to rest on the engine decks, or went in through open hatches. A dazzling white hell washed over the tanks and the bodies strewn about them.

A mountain of packing cases that could only contain new engines or whole transmissions received several more of the destructive grenades, and just two were sufficient for a stack of spare radiators. Molten copper and aluminum flowed as the bursting contents burned at two thousand degrees.

"Look for the machinery trucks. They're near here somewhere." It was almost impossible for Revell to make himself heard to Andrea, or for her to pass it on to the Grepos in the back. Generators and machinery still thundered on around them, and the crash and clatter of automatic fire was virtually continuous as all the weapons lashed out at every target that presented itself.

"They are there." Andrea smashed out the windscreen and sent a tracer-laced burst towards the dozens of machinists jumping from the row of heavy trucks and trailers.

Revell used a whole magazine as they motored along the line, pumping a shot into the radiator of each precious vehicle. As he did, he could hear the blast bombs Hyde's passengers were using tearing the guts out of the cabs and machinery decks. Lathes, drills and milling machines were smashed and toppled from their beds.

Panic was all around them. Time and time again, fleeing Russians would run straight into their fire. The terror and confusion was precisely what Revell had counted on. They were almost halfway round the perimeter road and not a shot had been fired against them so far.

The concussion from the grenades was punishing, threatening to burst their eardrums as waves of pressure from the blast bombs washed over them and rocked the vehicles. An explosive grenade Revell tossed at the side wall of a long wooden hut had an unexpected effect. The entire side of the light structure collapsed in a shower of planks and splinters, to reveal the interior of a radar and radio repair shop. It was too good a target to miss. Ordering Burke to stop, the major used two flame tubes on the racked

201

equipment and test benches. The single-shot weapons threw their charges of red phosphorus over everything, and the precious sets immediately began to explode in the heat.

As he sent the second on its way, before there was time to see the effect of the fountains of blazing chemicals, a bullet struck the roof of the car. It might have been careless shooting from Dooley, hosing bullets from the front of the truck as he fired the M60 from the shoulder, but in any case they had been stationary for too long.

Now they were passing welding and lubrication bays, and the sets of grease guns, gas bottles and arc welding kits, along with the AFVs parked by each, received their full share of attention. An eight-wheeled mobile crane and two armoured recovery vehicles parked nearby were given the same treatment.

Every blast wall and stack of stores they passed revealed new targets, but they brought fresh dangers as well. A burst of automatic fire came at them from between two Shilka flak tanks. They missed, and before the Russian could reload he was flushed from cover with a snap shot from a flame tube, and sent running with his clothes ablaze.

Thick smoke obscured the roof, dimming the powerful lights. It rose from a score of fierce fires in their wake. The pillars of curling flame marked their route, and it was that chain of beacons that gave away where they would be next.

Revell looked back to see that the truck was still with them. It was spitting bullets and incendiary materials from every side. As he turned back he barely caught a glimpse of the giant fork-lift truck bearing down on them, and then the shock of the collision threw him from his seat.

Twin broad spears pierced the unarmoured body-work of the car and he heard a terrible high pitched scream, then the fuel spilling from the ruptured tank ignited and the vehicle was filled with glaring red flame.

Intent on finding the other flak gun, Clarence paid only scant attention to the nearly continuous crash and roar of explosions from the camp. He was determined, and certain, that he would be successful, and experienced no surprise or elation when on the seventh IR sweep he found it.

Shortly afterwards, both anonymous patches re-solved into much more clearly defined configurations, and when he looked again through the image inten-sifier he was able to confirm that the Russian gun crews were removing the camouflage netting. He examined both with an expert eye. Neither was an easy target.

Gun crews, especially when they were in a pit, or behind sandbag walls as these were, were always difficult to hit. The most important member of the crew, the gun-layer, was inevitably behind armour, and the same shield gave cover to the loaders as they served the weapon. And when they weren't actually at the gun, they were forever bobbing up and down. It would have helped if his elevation had been greater than theirs, but if anything both gun-pits were a little above him.

The first he'd seen uncovered was a single mount, about . . . yes, 57mm. A weapon that carried a lot of punch, with a decent rate of fire. And the other . . . wasn't easy to make out. It was a multiple-barrelled mount, machine gun calibre by the look of it, most likely a quad 14.5mm. That was no toy either, it had a long reach and an incredible rate of fire if it was well served.

Which to tackle first? The crew of the 57mm piece had been first to uncover and prepare for action. He'd take that as an indication of their keenness to get into a fight, so he'd oblige them, but not with the sort of fight they were expecting.

The gun was elevating. The crew obviously believed the attack was coming from the air. Well, that suited him. Until they figured out, or were told the actual circumstances, they'd be whirling round and round and looking up. That would give him a perfect shot at their unprotected backs.

As though it were a match at Bisley, he carefully laid out his equipment on the groundsheet beside him and began his customary meticulous check on ammunition and rifle. In the next ten minutes or so he'd be finding fresh targets for them, adding further kills to his score.

As he worked he experienced a feeling of calm satisfaction. If he had just one regret about the whole business of being a sniper it was that his targets could never know, could never appreciate, the care he took over each shot. Unlike others whom he knew, he did not leave a trail of cripples and mental defectives in his wake. He aimed to kill and usually achieved just that; he could count on his fingers the number of times he had seen a man he'd hit crawl or stagger away and that was out of almost two hundred. It was a lot of lives, it was a pity it wasn't more.

*   *   *

Higher and higher soared the screaming as the impaled Grepos threshed about, making his agonies infinitely worse. Fire was everywhere, flaring about the inside of the car, licking from its windows.

Revell struggled up from the floor beneath the steering wheel. Through the flames he glimpsed a Russian major slumped flat-nosed against the bullet-holed glass front of the fork-lift's cab. Andrea was just scrambling clear, and together with Burke she reached for Revell to help him out.

The back of the car was hidden by swirling flame that engulfed the East Germans. As Revell was hauled clear the last of the petrol exploded with a roar, and a jet of fire licked after him, scorching his jacket and the fabric covering of his helmet. A blistered hand thrust from a window made a mute despairing appeal for help, and then was lost in the smoke and boiling flame.

"Into the truck." Letting go the last eight rounds in his magazine at a group of Russians trying to bring an unwieldy dismounted tank machine gun into action, Revell saw that the girl and driver had got in the back before jumping into the Ural's cab.

"We'll never make it the rest of the way round! Make for the main workshop. Move!"

Hyde had already seen a road-block being prepared ahead of them, and had swung on to one of the radial roads even before Revell shouted.

A Russian standing precariously on a blast wall got off several shots at the truck, before being hurled from sight by a well-aimed burst from Cohen. Another tried rolling a grenade, but fell with a bullet through his neck before the bomb exploded harmlessly behind the vehicle.

It was packed in the back of the truck, with everybody trying to keep low and fire at the same time. Bullets kept striking the bodywork and high canvas top above it, but no one was down, although there were splashes of blood on the floor and the inside of the tilt.

Hyde drove the truck straight into the huge repair shed, and braked to a halt in the middle of the thick walled structure. In long closely spaced rows on either side of them stood forty Soviet tanks, as well as some armoured missile and radar carriers.

The instant they stopped, a brisk fire opened up on them from a glass-walled office set high up on scaffolding at the far end of the workshop. Revell and Libby tumbled out to provide fire as Collins, Cohen and Rinehart set delay charges on each tracked vehicle, placing them inside open engine compartments or below turret overhangs. The electric motors of an overhead crane and the steel cradles holding replacement gun barrels received the same treatment.

It was as Collins sprinted across an open stretch of floor to reach a Ganef missile carrier that the unseen gunner on the balcony caught him. The bullets cut his legs from under him and he went down hard, lay still a moment, then gathered up the haversack he had dropped and crawled on.

Revell had only one magazine left; he'd been saving it for the generator on the way out. He snapped it into place, shouldered the weapon and fired a short burst.

On hitting the balcony the rounds broke up, scattering phosphorus. The pellets ignited immediately on exposure to the air. The remaining glass in the office walls shattered in the tremendous heat and the rapid clatter of the AKM ceased immediately. A moment later a figure appeared, smothered in rippling hoops of fire from the waist up. It beat the air with flame-dripping fingers, tottered forward and dropped over the edge to the floor twenty feet below.

Cohen was first to reach Collins, as he finished setting the last of his charges behind the Ganef's drive sprockets.

"OK kid, we're getting you out of here."

Collins didn't hear. He was in deep shock and both his legs were terribly shattered. Blood formed a large puddle about him, and marked his route from the middle of the floor. More of it soaked Cohen and Rinehart as they carried him to the back of the truck.

Revell slung the last satchel of explosives under the belly of an SA-8 missile launcher. "That's it. Let's go."

Hyde didn't look to see what speed they were doing, but when they hit the massive steel shutters that had been closed across the end doors of the drive-through workshop they crashed through them with hardly any check to their pace. The impact crushed in the Ural's front panelwork and friction-induced smoke began to pour from beneath a wheel arch.

A crowd of Russians scattered before them as they burst out and ploughed over them. Those not crushed beneath the wheels were mown down at point-blank range.

Seventy-five yards ahead lay the ramp by which they'd come in. Choking smoke swirled about them, now so thick that at times they could hardly make out the black-out curtain at its mouth.

Sixty yards to go, fifty, Hyde hunched over the wheel, willing greater speed from the engine. Forty and they had to make it, thirty, almost there, twenty, they'd almost done it, ten, nine . . .

Travelling fast, the jagged metal of the cab's front struck the material, smacking one flap aside, tearing another down as it caught on the projecting torn metal of a fender.

"Fuck it." There was no time for anything else. Libby threw up his hands to protect his face as the Ural thundered into the huge armoured recovery vehicle coming down through the outer doors.

Rugged as it was, the six-wheeler was no match for a modified T72, with its inches of armour and a weight more than four times that of the truck.

There was no room to pass, but Hyde tried throwing the Ural at the narrow gap between tank and wall to reduce the shock of impact. The tank's broad left track climbed on to and crushed the truck's engine before it stopped.

Revell found himself looking at the belly of the tank's pulley-and-hawser-adorned hull. The passenger door was tight against the wall and the other, distorted by the collision, was jammed. There was only one way out. One swing of his assault-rifle pushed out the windscreen, and then followed by Hyde and Libby he scrambled out on to the cab roof.

The uncomprehending crew of the ARV were climbing dazed from their vehicle. Hyde gave them no chance. His rifle barked three times and they tumbled back out of sight.

Revell jumped down and ran to the back of the truck where Dooley, blood streaming from a gash in his forehead, was helping the others out. A bullet zipped past him, very close.

"I'll fix those buggers." Hyde appeared, and pulled a

rocket launcher from the tangle of equipment on the floor of the truck.

"Take out the generator, that might do it."

Firing wild bursts from the hip Rinehart was already trying to do just that, but more bullets were coming at them, ricocheting from the concrete and striking sparks from the truck's chassis and rear axles.

Aboard the six-wheeler, Cohen was attempting to extricate Collins from beneath the pile of ammunition boxes. The major jumped on board to help. As they pushed the last aside they saw that the effort had been in vain. Collins stared at them with unseeing eyes.

"Join the others and have them start back for the skimmer." It took a hard shove to get Cohen moving.

Shouldering the launch tube, Hyde took careful aim. Bullets buzzed past him and smacked into the concrete at his feet, but he stood rock steady and kept the sights aligned on the big generator trailer sixty yards away. Only the top half of it was visible above a substantial sandbag blast wall, and that view was constantly being lost as smoke from burning drums of cable eddied about it.

Hyde gently squeezed the trigger and sent the black painted anti-tank rocket on its way. A few yards clear of the launch tube the projectile's main motor cut in and it raced towards its target.

They heard the crash of its impact, but smoke prevented them from observing precisely where. The arc lights remained on. Sergeant Hyde was reaching for another of the disposable launchers when the lights flickered, dimmed and faded.

"Will you look at that." Rinehart stood transfixed. "Hell must be like that."

It was a scene straight out of Dante's *Inferno*. The big underground complex was now only lit by the unchecked fires that raged within it. With the last of the machinery stilled, apart from the occasional bang of a round cooking off, the only noises came from the many trapped and wounded men. It was hard to breathe. The air was searing hot and filled with poisonous fumes from the fires.

A fresh flare-up from the direction of the knocked-out generator lit up the service road by which they'd escaped. It was filled with a hobbling, crawling mass of wounded.

All of them were making for the ramp. Rinehart brought up his rifle, but like Revell beside him in a similar pose, didn't fire.

The approaching men were pitiful. Only a few were groaning or making any complaint, but they served to highlight the silence of the majority. Shattered limbs, terrible burns and massive stomach wounds were all to be seen.

"We've done enough, let's get out." Skirting the truck, Revell was first to leap on to the front of the ARV completely blocking the ramp. He helped up Hyde and then extended his hand to Rinehart.

A scattering of shots came from somewhere among the wounded. They were being used as cover. One clipped Hyde's rifle and tore it from his grasp, another struck the armour at their feet and went on to bury itself in a thick baulk of timber attached to the hull-top.

Rinehart froze, dropped his assault rifle, then sprawled back to lay spreadeagled across the top of the recovery vehicle. A high velocity round had struck him between the eyes. His helmet could be heard falling

210

from ledge to ledge inside the hull.

At dangerously close range Revell put two shells into the truck's cab and, as they turned the crushed front of the Ural into a furnace, stepped back on to the recovery tank's engine deck and pumped shells in through each open hatch.

On reaching the top of the ramp they looked back. A wall of spitting chemical fire blocked it, and as they watched, the boiling fuel in the Ural's high capacity tank flared up and the over-stressed container split, sending a burning flood down the incline into the complex. There were no more shots, only screams.

Chapter Fifteen

Clarence was quite satisfied with his first shot. He'd watched as the gun-layer of the 57mm was lifted from his seat and laid out of sight below the rampart of sandbags. In a minute the body would have company.

The sniper settled himself behind his rifle again and waited. The non-stop concussion from the explosions in the hollow was no distraction, that was a discipline he had taught himself.

Another Russian was climbing into the seat. Clarence gave him a second to settle down and as the gun began to turn and dip, carefully pulled the trigger. He kept his eyes glued to the sight and waited— nothing. Confident, he maintained watch. Fully six seconds after he'd fired, his second victim slowly, almost gracefully, fell sideways and draped himself across the gun's breech.

There would be no third target, not at that gun. Four Russians jumped from the pit and ran. Clarence turned his attention to the machine gun mount, and swore quietly to himself. The barrels of the weapon had been dipped to bear on his hillside, and the gun-layer was hidden behind the close packed machinery of the guns themselves and the strips of vertical armour plate to either side. Flashes tipped each barrel and tracer soared across the gulf between the hills.

It had most probably been intended as morale booster, to give the crew the feeling they were doing something. But Clarence recognised that behind that random burst there lay an intelligent guess. Good: he enjoyed a duel and though not usually pitted against a flak gun, he wasn't concerned about the disparity in fire power. The extra risk would add spice to the contest. He fed a fresh round into the chamber and took a long time over sighting.

"Keep moving, keep moving." Revell caught up with the others and dragged them to their feet. "That lot was meant for Clarence, not for us!"

The tracer had started fires higher up the slope, away to their right. The circle of illumination they cast was rapidly expanding. Together Hyde and the major urged and shouted the others on, but there was no more speed to be got out of them. Dooley was having to help Libby who was trailing a leg, and Kurt clutched at his shoulder and seemed to slow with every pace.

Showers of sparks spiralled from the burning grass, starting fresh fires that spread towards them. Their way led between two patches of the flickering light, and a sudden increase in the strength of the breeze widened both to overlap and encompass the struggling group.

Another burst from the flak gun chewed the ground, throwing soil and clumps of grass over them. This time

214

no one took cover and the rate of progress up the hill increased.

At the instant the flak gun ceased firing there was the distinct crack of a single rifle shot from the crest. A hesitant answering burst from the heavy machine guns soared harmlessly into the sky and ended raggedly. Then there was silence.

Clarence didn't see or hear the others until Hyde nudged him with his boot. "Yes, alright, I'm coming." Reluctantly he pulled back from the sight and hurriedly began to pack. He hated having to leave without witnessing the effectiveness of his shot. All that he'd been able to see was a frontal view of the mount, its four barrels locked on him and unmoving. As they'd fired he'd drawn mental diagonals between the corners of the square marked out by the muzzle flashes and put a bullet into their imaginary intersection. If his memory of the captured guns he'd seen held good, then he'd put that bullet into the gun-layer's upper chest, a fraction below his voice box.

A series of sharp explosions made them stop and look back at the workshops. Each detonation came faster and louder than the preceding one. With a tremendous roar the whole huge yards-thick roof of the tank repair shed rose up on a pillar of boiling flame, punching effortlessly through the lightly constructed false roof of the camp and going a hundred feet into the night sky. It hung there for a moment, flame-trailing tank turrets cartwheeling through the air about it, dangling tassels of red-hot reinforcing rods, then fell back to complete the work of destruction.

Every inch of the refugee encampment was lit like day, as mushrooms of orange and yellow fire came out

215

of the gaping crater where the workshops had been.

Revell prodded the others into movement, forcing them to tear themselves away from the spectacle. He knew that every minute it took them to reach the skimmer was a minute less darkness for their journey back. And every passing moment also gave the nearest Russian units time to sort themselves out, figure what had happened and start to do something about it. They had to put distance, a lot of distance, between themselves and the havoc they had wrought on one of the Soviet Command's favourite outfits, and fast.

Libby was thinking along the same lines. "That was a hell of a thorough job we did, what's the betting the Ruskies will do as thorough a job on us if we're caught."

Maybe it was just because they had started downhill, but Hyde noticed an immediate and marked increase in the pace. .

"If we hadn't spent so much bloody time dodging trigger-happy Russian patrols on the way back to the Iron Cow we'd be bloody home by now." Burke thumped the bulkhead with his fist.

Dawn had caught them still six miles from their own lines, and with its coming a Russian Hind helicopter gunship had found them. It was the last of the relays that had sought them throughout the night.

Coming at them from behind, out of the rising sun, the first they had known of it was a near miss from an unguided air-to-surface missile. Ten more had plastered the ground around them as they bolted for the cover of a patch of devastated woodland. Four times the Hind made low level high speed sweeps across the area, blasting it with salvos of 57mm rockets, chewing up the trees and ground with long bursts from its gatling-type cannon.

"I can't get a shot at him through these damned trees." Fragments from more of the powerful warheads forced Hyde to duck back into the comparative safety of the turret's armour.

Libby, with his leg strapped stiffly, had been unable to get into the turret seat, and now he fumed and fretted as the sergeant took over his job.

"Wouldn't do any good anyway." At least he could offer advice. "Those buggers have titanium armour on the bits that matter. Best you could manage with that machine gun is to knock a few unimportant chips off him. You'll have to get in a good solid hit with the Rarden to bring him down."

"That's no cruddy learner out there." Dooley listened to the rattle of the 20mm cannon firing and the sound of the trees as they fell. "He ain't gonna come low enough or slow enough for you to get a poke at him with that."

Revell had been keeping a count. It wasn't exact, but he reckoned the Hind still had more than half its one hundred and twenty-eight unguided rockets left, plus the four big Swatter anti-tank missiles. If they stayed where they were, with the methodical pattern the Hind was working, it was only a matter of time before he scored a hit or a crippling near miss. If they left cover and made a run for it, he would have all the time in the world to put one of the devastatingly powerful anti-tank missiles into their hull, and that would be it.

Sunk down into his flak jacket, now slowly beginning to recover from the nausea of the long night ride, Cohen appeared to have shrunk. "So what do we do, sit here and wait for him to get lucky, and us to run out of ours? Please, don't think me pushy, but a way out of this shit I would like to hear."

Despite the noise and the danger, Andrea had fallen asleep on Clarence's shoulder. After two attempts to gently push her off the sniper had accepted the situation, even drawn a spare jacket over her. He had raised no objection when Hyde had mounted to the turret in his place.

Revell fought down an impulse, but couldn't completely subdue the urge he felt to separate them. It surged to the fore whenever his eyes strayed that way. "If we can't beat them, perhaps we can con them." He grabbed a signal pistol and box of flares. "Get everything burnable outside and I want two belts of machine gun ammunition; and somebody get me a couple of gallons of whatever it is this bus runs on."

Whipping the branches with the fierce downdraught from its five whirling blades, the gunship executed a tight turn at the end of its latest strafing run and began a sixth. Flame-tailed rockets flashed from the two pods slung from pylons beneath each stub wing set just behind the cabin, and the snouts of the cannon barrels below its nose showed a continuous blur of ragged-edged yellow as they maintained their high rate of fire.

The woods heaved and shook at the hammer blows. Revell crouched by the side of the skimmer and waited. A rocket detonated among a clump of holly bushes only twenty yards away, transforming the rich green leaves into flaming cinders that were scattered along with the branches. Debris still falling about him, Revell

218

ran to the pile of kerosene-soaked rags and fired a flare into them. He felt the sudden heat on his face as the bonfire instantly ignited, sending black smoke billowing up through the trees. For good measure he flung the box of flares into the fire, then sprinted back to the skimmer as ammunition in the belts began to cook off and send multi-hued tracer in every direction.

"He's buying it, the fucker is buggering off. No, he's not, what the hell is he doing?" Dooley watched from the doorway as the helicopter did a half turn, and then hovered. "The bastard, he's coming down, he's going to drop off infantry to come and make sure of us."

"Full power!"

Burke had already anticipated the major's order, and the craft was surging forward even as Revell jumped on to the ramp. With it still lowered, the skimmer thundered through the trees towards the spot where the chopper was coming down, and reached it as the first of a squad of heavily armed Russian infantry was preparing to jump from its side door even before the wheels were on the ground.

Burke threw the motors into full reverse thrust and the Iron Cow slewed to a stop only fifty yards away. Hyde opened up with the Rarden. All of the first clip were hits, one shell plunging in through the side of the machine just below the weapon operator's forward cockpit, and two more scoring direct hits on the main cabin. At the same time Revell and Dooley hosed light automatic fire from the ramp and cut down two Russians who had fallen from the cabin doorway and were making frantic wild jumps to get back on board as the gunship soared up beyond their reach.

At maximum elevation Hyde managed to score one

more hit, on the port engine housing, just to the rear of the pilot's cockpit. Oily smoke poured from the damaged turboshaft's exhaust stack and the machine began to pitch nose down.

Two hundred feet above the clearing, a big bubble of flame came from the open cabin and was sliced into streamers by the blades. Its dive steepened and a pin-wheeling body and pieces of equipment fell from it as it turned on to its side before plunging into the trees.

Revell handed the XL6 rifle back to Libby, who'd dragged himself to the doorway to look at the spectacle. "I don't think I'll be needing this again. OK everyone, back to your seats."

Andrea sat next to Clarence again, and pulling the jacket over herself, nestled against him once more. The sniper affected not to see the look Revell gave him, as he rearranged the material to cover her better, and then left his arm resting lightly across her shoulders.

A leering grin creased Kurt's dirty face, but a glance at Revell and he said nothing.

"What's the heading, Major?" Burke hit the control to bring the ramp up.

"Due west." Revell felt he hardly had the strength left to speak, as if the last drop of energy had been drained from him. "Let's go home."

"According to TASS you burned down a whole fucking refugee camp." Ol' Foul Mouth lounged back in his chair.

"Just the part they were using." Major Revell had washed and shaved, and he still felt a thousand years older than the antique desk the colonel sat behind.

220

"Yeah, well that's as maybe, but because of the chance of a fucking stink from all the shitty liberals and fellow-travelers back home there ain't gonna be no press, no medals, no hoo-ha."

"Then what's our version, sir." That last word almost stuck in his throat.

"We don't know nothin', sweet F.A. Our reply to the Reds' accusation is to say that if independent observers are let in, they'll see we didn't do it. But of course the Ruskies ain't gonna allow that, because those same busy-bodies will see what's left of the workshops. So we score that way. Shit, I know it ain't much, but there's times, like over the '80 Olympics, when just getting up their hairy nostrils is a victory." Lippincott shuffled the papers on his desk to no particular purpose. "Eh, those Limeys still around?"

"Their sergeant is busy trying to find transport to get them back to their unit." The question seemed to have no supplement. Revell hoped the interview was over. "If that's all, Colonel . . ."

Ol' Foul Mouth looked up sharply. "Don't be in such a fucking hurry, Major, and tell the British the same, I got another little job for you . . ."

GREAT BOOKS

E-BOOKS

AUDIOBOOKS

& MORE

Visit us today

www.speakingvolumes.us